Robert Holland, R. A., began his spectacular career in the late 1940s. His artistic career began in the Dundee Studios of the famous book and comic illustrator, Dudley D Watkins. It was here that he met and later married the English society artist Amy Beatrice Robinson (second cousin of Heath Robinson). They moved to London in April 1950, where they jointly formed a studio, and he became the resident political cartoonist of *The Reynolds News*. Through contacts at their studio he then became set designer for many classic Ealing film comedies including *Hue and Cry* and *The Lady Killers*. In a dramatic change of career during the later years of the decade he became a well known television personality (in 1959 his popularity was second only to MacDonald Hobley and a character actor in many films alongside his screen partner, Ian Carmichael. Throughout the 1960s he pursued a multicoloured career, during which time he became recognised as one of England's leading book illustrators. He won the coveted Academy Hurlant award for his illustrations for Joe Orton's posthumous novel, *Hair to Toe*. He was a nominee for an Academy Award for his expressionist set designs which he created for William Burroughs' and Anthony Balch's film, *Towers Open Fire*. Today he lives in Paris where he is art editor of the prestigious avant-garde quarterly, *Gazette du Bon Ton*. His illustrations for *Lord of the Rings* were previewed in *Harper's Bazaar* early in 1980. Later this year his highly ambitious edition of *Les Choses de Paul Poiret*, containing over 200 illustrations and paintings, will be released as a strictly limited edition.

THE SCREWRAPE LETTUCE is the seventh book in
the Savoy Collected Editions of Jack Trevor Story's
famous novels. The other books in the series are . . .

The Albert Argyle Books
Live Now, Pay Later
Something for Nothing
The Urban District Lover

TV Tie-In
Jack on the Box

The Classic Novel Filmed by Alfred Hitchcock
The Trouble With Harry

And
Man Pinches Bottom
The Money Goes Round
One Last Mad Embrace
Wind in the Snottygobble Tree

JACK TREVOR STORY
The Screwrape Lettuce

SAVOY BOOKS
In association with
NEW ENGLISH LIBRARY
TIMES MIRROR

Copyright Jack Trevor Story 1979, 1980

Published by Savoy Books Ltd.,
279 Deansgate, Manchester M3 4EW,
England, under the author's original title

First published by Gerald Duckworth
& Co. Ltd., as "Up River"

Cover artwork: Harry Douthwaite

Interior illustrations: Robert Holland

Printed by: S.E.T. Ltd., Manchester

ISBN 0 86130 038 6

For my lady Elaine
and the rivers
of the summers of
those years
and to the memory
of that dog

1

Saturday tea times Caroline often went to Mrs Glen's in Hampstead Gardens. She was now looking quite earnestly for a husband but was usually forced to accept lovers. She had about four ports of call—her expression—in her time off from the bankruptcy building, the others being old digs or old workmates or old Oxford friends now in professions.

"This is Jek. Jek's a writer from South Efrica. Jek, I want you to meet Caroline. She's en Official Receiver's exeminer, if you know whet thet is."

"The arsehole of the nation," said Caroline. "Bankruptcy."

Alison Glen ran an open house for wandering compatriots, particularly those fighting apartheid or with plans to murder Vorster, the present prime minister. Caroline had first come to Alison with one of her barristers. Caroline Latimer had legal gentlemen and was not yet recovered from the one who was going to marry her, Warren Morgan.

"Warren's on the radio in half an hour. I don't want to hear the bastard again but I have my fucking self-denigrating compulsion. One doesn't give up until one is totally destroyed, I believe. It's that Inter-action squatter case in Kentish Town."

"Ceroline and Warren were together for how long was it, Ceroline? Five years?"

"I was a cunt," Caroline explained to the new young writer. "If you can have lady cunts. I fed him and he fucked me for five years. When he had to choose between me and his flea-bitten alsatian he chose the dog. Is your clock right, Alison? He's on Radio 4."

"Tune the radio, Jek. Don't let Ceroline frighten you. She's

11

quite sweet really, except on her Warren days. You shouldn't watch for him es you do, dear." Her real concern was for the alarmed young writer. Caroline was kneeling into his crutch through her long gypsy skirt, her almost empty Harrods bra on his ear, her thin Surrey nostrils flaring manically as she listened for the old blood-stirring voice.

By seven o'clock it was clear to Caroline that Jack was going to sleep with a little runtish girl in jeans who was on holiday from Durban. She had sat in one of Alison's club armchairs without saying a word and then suddenly Jack had taken her off to the pub.

Caroline said: "I'm talking too much, aren't I?"

"Yis, dear," said Mrs Glen.

"Anyway, I can't stand men who wear anoraks. One likes to see a man dress like a man, not like some Orwellian cipher."

"Tim wears suits," said Alison Glen. They were two small ladies; Alison prematurely elderly and related physically and genetically to the Fabians' founding mother, Beatrice Webb.

Caroline brightened at mention of Tim. "Yes, I know he does. And waistcoats. He's really rather my type. Striped shirts, briefcase, rolled brolly. I suppose it must be hereditary. Not bowler hats, though. One draws the line at caricature."

"How's your father's impotence now?" Alison inquired.

The conversation got on to familiar lines. Other people drifted in. Not Tim. Caroline began to look a little strained. She liked to sleep with somebody on Saturday nights, pretend it was Warren. Warren was now living with some married bitch and her two kids and his mangy alsatian in a squat in Hackney—mean bastard. His voice sounded full of sex. She knew deep down there would be nobody else as long as she lived. While she was still young and on the circuit she would get fucked and after that the long nothing. She had to face it; men did not immediately think of bed when they looked at her.

"Caroline ..:" Alison Glen called from a group in the window. Keeping people included was part of her facility. "Show them your pistol, dear. Harry won't believe you carry a loaded gun."

Caroline lifted her big Indian shop bag from her feet, rummaged in it and came out with a Browning automatic. She raised it in almost the same movement, released the safety catch with the forefinger of her other hand and fired. A heavy bearded man caught pruning a cutting from the window fuchsia screamed like a rabbit. There was a beginning of nervous laughter, then silence. The mixed group were staring at the portrait of Vorster over the mantelpiece. It was full of bullet holes. Amid the amusement and the explanations two black Africans—one called Onyx from Johannesburg now lecturing in Canterbury, his friend a porter at the British Museum—got up and left and never came back.

"Tell them about your dangerous jobs," said Mrs Glen.

Caroline Latimer had been attacked three times since graduation and never for her body. With two degrees, one honours, she had first of all taught at a top people's crammers where she had been set upon by the idiot son of a cabinet minister whom she had been forced to swear at more or less constantly. With four stitches in her head and a fractured nose she had given up the school and started a field job for social services. Here she had run foul of a man who believed she was having an affair with his eleven-year-old son—one finger broken and a strained back from getting knocked down stairs. Lastly, there was a straight punch on the jaw from one of her bankrupts.

"We have a chaperone now at Thomas More. Partly to protect me, partly to prevent anyone jumping. One is forced by statute to question bankrupts at a rather privy level, as it were. Still, I must say I enjoy it. We all do. It gives one an enormous feeling of power. Particularly after battling in a crowded train to get there. One can hit back. Bankrupts are terrified you're going to discover hidden money and take it away from them. One gets tuned to lies. Once they've signed a lie they can go to prison. I've put five in prison so far, and I think I've almost got another. By the way, Alison, do you known an Amy Farmer? I think that's her married name."

"Should I?"

"You remember Bubbles?"

Five people present in the room remembered Bubbles.

"And do you remember the woman who took her baby?"

Mrs Glen explained to strangers: "Bubbles is Indian from Cape Town. She was with me for a year until I got her a place in Highgate. She hed a bleck baby by en Efrican father. Thet's why she couldn't go home, do you see. The state would separate them. Well, I don't hev to tell you. Then her mother died and Bubbles had to go beck to her deddy—yis! Yis Caroline! Farmer. Amy, thet was it. I met her once. Hedn't she lost a child?"

"In a way. In fact several."

The partial strangers in the room, which most of Mrs Glen's expatriates were, made a token pretence to start their own conversations at this intimate turn of events in an absent friend's life. The competition from the lurid official-receiver mind was overwhelming.

"She had three abortions on the trot. You can't claim for abortions. They cost much more than babies, yet you get no allowances. Still, three little foetuses down the sewage. One's mind simply revolts. There are those of us who wouldn't say no to one healthy fucking baby and can't bleeding well fucking well do any fucking thing about it. One's mind does tend to boggle."

"All by the same father?" asked Mrs Glen. "The ebortions, I mean."

"Then of course when she wanted a baby she found it was no go. Any intelligent woman would have known that. That's why she adopted Bubbles' little black boy."

Several people began to understand the conversation.

"God knows what kind of mother she makes. Something like mine, I should think. A right bloody vegetarian whore."

"More tea anyone?" asked Alison Glen.

"They won't kill animals but they'll put a knife in anyone moral. Friends of the fucking earth, vegetarians, liberals, sending their kids to be destroyed at freak freedom schools. From A. S. Neill to Oxford. We had to lie in bed with our parents while they copulated. Ride a cock horse to a climax. By the time one reaches puberty the conventions are so forbidden you dream about them. One does, I mean. One's coevals and one's self constitute a generation of virginal cock-suckers."

"Does anyone know anything about the new mandate for South West Africa?"

This was the summer of crisis. Youngsters on their obligatory European tour were rushing home to rescue their parents from massacre and worse. Raymond and Tad were going to Athens. Raymond had been watching Caroline and making more sense of her buttocks and powerless bare arms than of her conversation.

"Bankruptcy is a criminal act as I understand it. Correct me if I'm wrong." This was Dr Don Muller, a consultant physicist. Even on such a hot night as this he had managed to remain correct in his dark suit and tie, reaching, like most middle-class colonials abroad for proof of ruling status even among these dissidents. He and his actress wife had brought a bottle of whisky and a rolled umbrella. He was waiting for Caroline Latimer to reassure him in his social prejudices. "Bankrupts are crooks, aren't they?" Success held less satisfaction in a world where failure was more or less okay.

The telephone rang and somewhere a voice called out and another said it was Caroline's mother.

"Tell her to piss off. No, let me tell her." A moment later the little legal lady's voice screamed through the house and across Hampstead Gardens.

"FUCK OFF! FUCK OFF, MUMMY!"

Dr Muller said: "She hes a remarkable mind, Alison."

"Fentestic. Play some more music, Raymond—"

"Fuck off, you nosey cow. Where did you get this fucking number? I told you never ring me at my friends' houses. You piss up my life. You pissed up Warren. You pissed up David. Every man I have, you piss it up. All that middle-class fucking greed. Cross-examining them about their prospects. Fuck off, mummy."

Raymond de Freitas chorded a new love song on his guitar,

but it sounded like an obligato to the telephone conversation in the hall.

"Mother, you are incorrect. I do not usually come down to Guildford on a Saturday. I do not usually do anything. I do what I fucking like. I come down to Guildford when there is piss all else to do or when I am fucking skint. Shut your poxy mouth, mummy. You are being repaid for my education—shut up. What? I don't care who you've got in to meet me. I am not going to marry your rich old men. I don't care if he's Toc H himself. What? You said he was a Mason—oh, fuck off, mother, do. You've always used our bodies to get your own way. Wilfred a ladies' hairdresser at twelve. Julia and I were tossing off old men when we were ten—yes! Yes! People don't forget, mummy! Those fucking town councillors when you were trying to get the road widened for your Armstrong Siddeley— what? No! I am not coming home. Fuck your own Mason ..."

"She went to Summerhill," Mrs Glen was explaining to the room. "They talk like this to their parents. They're friendly, really. It's jist different. Less inhibited—"

"It's not your business. I live my own life, mother. So does Julia, so does Daddy. What? Don't lie! They never give you an inch. Julia's married, Daddy's impotent and I'm on the game— yes! Yes! I want a baby. I am playing Russian roulette with my vagina—and listen! Stop telling people I'm a judge, mother. I am an examiner in bankruptcy. A civil servant. I did mean it. You might control my inheritance from grandma but you can't make me take the pill. I fuck every weekend and send in urine samples once a fortnight—Don't you dare! Don't you dare! If you put someone in my room I'll set fire to the house. Who? Chinese? You fuck-pig, mummy! You bleeding fucking fuck-pig! That's not going to give Daddy the horn ..."

"Family heppy?" inquired Mrs Glen, when Caroline finally returned.

"Something's eating mummy's guppies," she said.

DIARY OF A MAGISTRATE

After the telephone call I took some fresh tea in a flask out to C. H. in the garden. Which vaguely irritated him, I think, because he was probably on the point of making tea an excuse to break off work and come indoors out of the sun. That incredibly hot weekend he had to prepare his geraniums for a BBC camera crew. Most of our garden and quite a lot of the house is really a camera mock-up for this programme or that article. The bathroom was a before-and-after for Woman's Own.

"Was that Weenie, darling?" My husband gives the impression that he's nervous of me, but really this is a part of his general humility and diffidence when in the presence of people who are not being interviewed or scripted. Real people put performers at a disadvantage. This I have often noticed when people like David Jacobs or Magnus Magnusson have been in to supper or drinks. Magnus, particularly, goes into the wallpaper; I sat through a three-course dinner at one of Jane's Radio Times get-togethers without identifying him. He was shocked but not disbelieving when several well-known people recounted incidents of police brutality which they had experienced or witnessed. One believes such things happen, but not in Chiswick.

"You had a lot to talk about." A sign of would-be eccentrics is that they wear hats. Even on his afternoon radio programmes, 'C. H. Latimer Exactly,' C. H. wears his droopy gardening hat. It is for him what sand is for an ostrich, I think. He is a terribly nice man and reasonable almost to screaming point. He believes that his hat hides this. Words like 'liberal' and 'tolerant' and 'radical' are inside that hat, but they don't show even one iota. His facility, shared with Roy Plomley on Desert Island Discs, is for making normal people sound daring.

"Believe me, I do understand that, indeed I do," C. H. will say when somebody has said, 'I believe in God' or something equally unremarkable. And Mark, his producer, will tell me, fervently: "You know, C. H. is so good at drawing people out!" This is no criticism, simply an explanation of his hat. It's orange. "Yes, Caroline was chatty," I told him. I poured him some tea and he sat on the Habitat folding-stool. My daughter is much more outgoing on the telephone. We get closer somehow. He said: "Is she coming down?"

"Yes. She says she isn't."

"She'll be here, then. Very obtuse, Davis said. Davis met her. Did I tell you Davis met her? Our Features Editor—did you know he's come home from Bangkok? His wife died."

"That's interesting," I said. "Did he like Weenie?"

"Ah! Now that's the sixty-four-thousand dollar question!"

He has these BBC clichés; I doubt whether he knows where they come from. "But what did he say about her?"

"Rather a funny thing, actually. Your daughter's full of modicums and boggles." Like her daddy, I thought. But I said: "She likes the idea of letting her bedroom to a Chinese student. She thinks it will cheer the place up."

C. H. looked up at me with his confused look; he likes things to be absolutely straightforward to the point of utter banality. He said: "I hope Weenie doesn't know why she's coming here?"

"I haven't told her if you haven't."

"You know I never mention personal things. To Julia, perhaps. But Weenie is very conformist. I don't feel happy about that magazine. Somebody outside the family knows about our problem." Some unkind person had taken out a year's subscription for C. H. to a rude magazine which had started arriving in a plain envelope. I thought it was possibly Weenie.

"You ought to have an affair with some talkative secretary," I said. We all know, don't we, that daddy's inability is all in the mind. This is not to dismiss his sickness but to compound it. On the second cup of tea C. H. had started to rock, gently. And this first sign of autism is where Caroline's trouble all began when she was Weenie. The rocking-chair in the brain is natural for the world-weary, but the autistic—rather horrifying I think— are the babies who have inherited old age.

Through their incomprehensible furies you offer them some news about the tropical fish pond. And this they understand. It is a rocking-chair.

2

Raymond's room was not much more than a bowman's slot in a Gothic castle by the heath. When Caroline Latimer opened her legs fully she touched both walls. It was partly this and partly that she could smell Alison's vaginal spray on his beard that stopped her wanting to participate. Being a musician, Raymond was sensitive to this and stopped riding up and down. "I'm awfully sorry," she said. "I seem to have rather lost the mood." He said: "Do you mind if I finish?" She said: "Well, I'd really rather you didn't. If you don't mind. There's nothing worse than cold semen inside one. Well, I mean, one expects a modicum of mutual fire. Why don't you play one of your tunes and then we'll see."

Raymond de Freitas sang a song of the bushmen, of the lakes in the highlands, west from Durban. A song of Luras, a black girl who could not become his wife. Caroline saw him as a silhouette, his back pressed against the small slot of a window, the big jumbo guitar held almost vertical against his naked body; they sat facing each other like two people in a small oblong boat. Their bottoms were resting on a plastic sleeping bag on top of a folding chromium-framed campbed. Between the rhythm of the words and the arpeggioed chords, Raymond drummed a roll of fingertips on the soundboard. His penis, under the guitar, Caroline was relieved to notice, had drooped and a small droplet of come cobbled the hairs around it.

He sang:

"Luras. Looma looma looma. In my hand
I hold seed and plant and bloom. Ah,

In our love, we hold our future in the Rand ..."

There followed eight bars modulating through the subdominant chord to the relative minor. As it came up to E7, ready for the next stanza, Caroline Latimer said: "Could we have a bath somewhere?"

"Beg peddon?" said the minstrel. He lay aside the guitar and wiped his cock on the back of his hand, self-consciously. He was really in good voice tonight and he was wishing this short-sighted bluestocking with no tits would piss off home.

"A nice warm bath. I feel quite mucky. Trouble is I haven't got a tooth brush." She was applying the law of reversals that lovers use; taking his shortcomings to herself.

In fact Raymond did not need all this. He pulled on his denim shorts and took her up the road, she clasping her underclothes in a plastic carrier printed with Sam Cook. They appeared to break and enter somebody's house, going first to a big kitchen where Raymond put on an electric kettle; then to the bathroom.

"Is this absolutely all right?"

"Yis," he said.

She sat in a strange lavatory and made herself thoroughly comfortable. There was a card on the door asking people to keep the place clean and pleasant. To take the edge off the fascism of this, another notice said: "Roses are reddish, violets are blueish. But for Christmas we'd all be Jewish." As she went to wipe her arse, a slip of paper fell out of the toilet roll reminding the users to get a replacement. Caroline Latimer began to feel curiously at home. She felt that the people who usually sat on this seat would like her. She got screwed but she didn't get liked very much.

When her bowel had stopped moving, Caroline Latimer waited several minutes, knowing it would move once more. She passed the time bombing the lino pattern with spittle. Soon her bowel moved again and then she was contented.

She always did this. In a strange place this was the only way to calm her down. Sit her on the pottie. There was a boy, Otto, at High Wick, who

20

would achieve the same security by wee-weeing into his shoes. One day when C.H. and I had driven up to St Albans to visit Weenie, Otto was standing outside the home in Cell Barnes Lane, not crying and not laughing but just staring along the lane at nothing. His parents had driven away an hour ago.

It touched me so deeply that I got their number and rang them up sometimes. Twice we visited them at Sawbridgeworth and once they came to us in Guildford. Then it dropped off. I think it's better not to make a club of personal disasters. I wouldn't belong to the autistic parents' society. Autistic kids are a bloody bore and their parents are worse.

Although it is widely advertised by the intelligent journalists that nobody knows what causes autism, whether it is genetic or due to pre- or post-natal treatment, most people who think they're in the know blame parents. For being too old, or neglectful or simply round the twist. We are cross-examined by our insane child's doctors. I have made no secret of my own guilt so far as Caroline is concerned. When I was a child in Newcastle, New South Wales, I was diagnosed mentally disturbed. It was a horrifying phase. I was fat, nearly blind and with a disgusting complexion. On my sixteenth year I turned into a beautiful princess. This worried the doctors even more. The other thing I told Dr Maschler at High Wick was about Caroline's squint. I caused it by hanging a button over her cot all the time she was a tiny baby. This is a frightful thing to confess and may be part of my own insanity, but the reason seemed rational enough at the time. I had fallen in love with somebody and gone to bed with him twice. When I found myself pregnant there was some doubt in my mind. C.H. has a slight squint; Weenie had not. Until I gave it to her. There was a very ironic and inconsequential aftermath. Years later I met Jay—that was this publisher I had been working for in London—and he was cross-eyed. Wearing special glasses.

Now if you add all these things together they come to the square root of minus one—which is nothing. An abstract lubricatory factor, once known as J-notation and now the German I-factor in mathematics. A button, in fact, hanging on a cot; it cancels out once you know all the other variables. The worst day of my life I spent lying on my back in the grass on Hampstead Heath at nine months pregnant with Caroline. I knew that Jay could see me. At five in the afternoon He came out and got into his car and drove away fast. It was the only cry for help I ever made.

Now I am autistic enough to know autistic people. We talk too much sometimes, gabble, or fall into unbroken silence as though ice has formed; we *swim around underneath it frantic for a hole. If in apparent lucidity a subject begins to escape, thought diffusing, our volume goes up—the gabble is louder, unintelligible. In an artist working at his own pace in utter seclusion the result is illumination amounting almost to genius—but with gaps. William Blake was autistic, loaded with the autistic child's geriatric innocence. In the midst of their best work they become unintelligible. Their teeth drop out.*

When she came out of the lavatory Raymond de Freitas had her bath ready—warm, not hot, for a sweating night and perfumed lavender with plenty of stiff high foam and bubbles.

"Don't run your water out," he requested. "I'll edd some more to it."

They were talking softly though the water had been rushing like Niagara. He watched her drop the long dress around her feet and step out of it, held her hand when she stepped into the bath. She said: "Who lives here?" He said: "Heven't a clue." Then subsided her alarm with: "They're Efrican. Frinds of frinds." Caroline Latimer said: "That leaves one yet another remove and starkers—better lock the door."

The kettle started whistling in the kitchen, taking Raymond away. She stepped out and bolted the door after him. Sex and bathing were two different things since the little soapy penetrations of Summerhill.

Caroline Latimer was standing near the kitchen sink with her dress rolled up to her belly. She was letting the cold tap run fiercely so that it splashed her and made her catch her breath.

"I always do this," Caroline would say. "At home, I mean. Mummy does it. We used to do it at Summerhill. Girls and boys mixed. All pubic and hairy by fourteen. I tried to introduce it at Ox. One met such contrasting moral codes at St Anne's …"

Because of the sound of the water Dobbin came in now without being heard. She noticed him almost instantly; he was naked and didn't attempt to cover himself, even instinctively.

"Oh dear," said Caroline. She was reaching for a roll of kitchen paper, tearing some off, padding at her wet crutch and belly and legs. "Do you live here?" In the bathroom Raymond could be heard singing more of his veldt love song. The onus seemed to be on her, conversationally. "I'm afraid I'm rather trespassing. I'm with Raymond. From down the road. You're South African, aren't you?" she added, as if claiming amnesty.

"No. Arforshire."

Caroline Latimer lowered her dress. This simple action seemed to embarrass him and he backed away: "I'll get covered up."

"Do you want some tea?" she called after him and he called back that he did and she heard a door open and close. While she had the chance she reached into the Sam Cook carrier and got out some knickers, which she slipped on. When he returned, wearing what appeared to be a pillow case, they were both more relaxed. He offered her his hand:

"Ben Dobbin."

"Oh? I'm Caroline Latimer. The tea's just made. Do you take sugar and milk? I expect it's your stuff. I'm sorry."

"Tharsallright."

From this one omnibus word she now worked out that he had previously said that he came from Hertfordshire. Ben Dobbin, the name, sounded like a stuffed toy. A horse, that was it. He looked like a kindly shire horse; a heavy forelock of black hair, a red countryfied face with freckles, breasts almost qualifying for a bra, but hairy. He was about five feet ten and appeared to have a good figure, though she suspected that a beer belly would roll out as soon as the light went out. What endeared him to her was a solitary tattoo, Margie, across his heart. Caroline Latimer had considered having Warren tattooed at womb level.

"We've been to Mrs Glen's," said Caroline, when they sat across the corner of a red plastic kitchen table top.

"Ohar?" said Dobbin.

Her researching habit took over. "Are you the landlord?"

"No. I just got one room same as the others. Share kitchen and bathroom and loo. Landing, telephone."

"Who are these South Africans?"

"Dunno. Might be Ann and Graham. They were the last. Went six months ago."

"Do you let their friends go on using your bathroom?"

"Better than finding strangers in the kitchen." This came with a slow smile which now, belatedly, evoked the cold water splashing on her belly, bringing them together.

He said: "Why don't you bring it in my room? Listen to the music."

"Do you mind?" Caroline Latimer said, brightly.

And as they went, carrying their tea cups, she said: "We'll keep an ear out for Raymond or he'll wonder where I am."

And later, Caroline Latimer said: "Do you mind switching off the light a moment, Dobbin—he'll think I've gone ..." She had finished with Raymond.

"One has a distinct feeling of being a widow after being deserted by a fucking bastard like Warren Morgan," said Caroline Latimer to her new friend. "That's why I'm letting you do this to me."

Raymond de Freitas had bathed and cleaned his teeth and drunk his tea and sung one more verse of his love for a black lady. Caroline lay on the bed with Dobbin in the dark, their hands upon each other. The song went, guitarless:

"Luras. You may be raped, no white avowal.
Your grandma, was raped by Baden Powell."

And then they heard him call: "Ceroline! Hev you gone beck?" And they heard him mutter, thankfully: "Fecking good riddence!" A window slid up and down as he broke out of the house. Caroline Latimer cleared her throat.

Dobbin said: "I believe I know him. Hans Andersen we call him." "I call him a prick," Caroline said. Dobbin said: "You're not engaged then?" "How old are you, Dobbin?" she asked. "Forty-five and a bit," he said. "I thought so. Engaged! Parents say things like that. My fucking whore of a mother. Trying to palm me off with a Mason. Fucking small-town bourgeois Ku Klux Klan."

Caroline then said: "Do you want me, Dobbin?"

"Yesacourse."

She imagined him adding "milady". She felt like Lady Chatterley must have felt in the stable with her gamekeeper. It pleased her, this swift establishing of a bed relationship on a surname basis. There arose in Caroline Latimer a rich enjoyment of all the things she most despised in her middle-class, stockbroker-belt Surrey parents with their dogs and the daughter at the Beeb. She had gone one better; Caroline had got a human fucking horse: a Dobbin. She saw herself taking him home, leading him up the garden path on a rein. She would put him out to graze in the garden of the mock-Tudor semi-detached. That's Dobbin, Caroline's centaur. He would go rather well with the plastic goldfish pool and C. H. Latimer's peacocks. She could see the long cock dragging on the petunias when he was at stud.

"What do you do?" she asked.

"What, me?"

There is no reply to this evasion and it was not in Caroline Latimer's legal nature to make one.

"Orsorsafings," he said then.

She had already noticed that when Ben Dobbin was becoming passionate his enunciation suffered. There was a certain rough tenderness about his physical advances. His mouth tasted wholesome and fingers traced her eyebrows and gently massaged her temple as if she had complained of a headache; as if life was too much. She found this extremely endearing and as a reward she opened her legs. One of his hands ran down into her crack and stayed there, motionless.

"I think you're lovely," he said.

She said, softly: "Do you, Dobbin?"

She reached down and took his hand from her vagina, brought it up to her mouth and dribbled spittle along his forefinger. Then she returned it to its place. He used the lubrication as intended and at the same time brought his belly over to hers and she felt the hard penis lying across her groin. She played with it for a moment. Then on an impulse she went down on him and took the acorn into her mouth, began the rituals that had started with the Guildford town councillors. When they were ready they joined, working together at a steady, controlled rhythm, determined to make it last.

"Slow down," she murmured. "Come right out with each stroke. That's right. That's beautiful. Think of icicles."

"Gojamarvellous," he said.

"Am I, Dobbin?" said Caroline Latimer.

At the moment of her first climax she closed her eyes and imagined that her lover was Warren Morgan, the solicitor.

There was something wrong with Warren Morgan. Even C.H. noticed it. We were both at first swept off our feet and were left after he had gone with a silence between us. Instead of that natural probing comment. You don't want to say anything unkind about somebody you have just been laughing with.

"He seems all right."

"Yes. Weenie is gone on him."

Your autistic daughter being gone on somebody was no guarantee of anything. Rather a chilling thought in fact. Autistic people cannot give love. They need it. Their life is a continual shopping for love. I know cabbages in institutions and I know a headmistress and I know my daughter at the law courts and I know myself. We attract people who will ask for nothing and be content to graze. They will see your weaknesses and try to exploit them, only to find that they are not weaknesses at all but simply more walls. The autistic are battling the wrong way through a maze, followed by their well-meaning unloved ones.

I got out. When my babies were born I was born with them. They say things are not inherited, but they are. Everything we are is inherited. We are rubbing shoulders with horrors of every sort in different degrees. Kindness is a symptom, cruelty is a symptom and so is smiling. Fury is a symptom. Keeping her furies intact Caroline fought her way out of the maze; from High Wick to Cell Barnes to Rudolph Steiner to Summerhill. Luckily for her she had a mind that took examinations in its stride and understood the minds behind the papers. She has, fortunately, inherited her father's conventional establishment thinking, his limited university vocabulary, his clichéd terms of reference. Caroline can sound like a law book. So can Warren.

"They've got a lot in common ..."

Do you, Warren? Did you, Warren? Could you, Warren?

This is her most endearing Weenieism. Anything said to her she has the ability of lobbing back with the speaker's name added as a kind of affectionate compliment. It gives one's decisions and deliberations of even the most trivial nature some subtle extra weight. "I think I'll go to bed." "Shall you, mummy?" It is the autistic's need to communicate at every second in order to stop the ice forming. This need to keep the engine ticking over and disguise their inhibited social faculty produces the world's worst bores. When Caroline turns up with her rolled umbrella and twin set and a token bottle of vin rouge, we know the weekend is finished.

"She ought to get married," says poor C.H.

But if she doesn't turn up I have to phone her to reassure her that she is needed. A fairly normal family in other words.

"You're still hard, Dobbin."

"Am I?"

"Gosh. It really is astonishing."

"Do you want to go again?"

"Oh, no thank you. One gets just the tiniest bit sore. I'll be all right in the morning I expect."

"I'm on early duty tomorrow," said Ben Dobbin.

They both realised that an admission of some sort had been made. Her immediate assumption was that Dobbin was a policeman and on this came awful racial apprehensions. The sexual pleasures of the past hour must be illegal. She had been led into a trap. It had to do with breaking and entering the house; Dobbin's sudden appearance naked in the kitchen when she was splashing her front. Even her comfortable shit now seemed illegal to Caroline Latimer. In her mind she searched the torts.

"Are you, Dobbin?" she said. And she said: "Do you work on Sundays?"

"Some on some orf."

His words were beginning to close up again and she realised that she was still holding his erection; nothing of their mutual unease had affected it. Now he slipped his arm under her shoulders and rested her face into his chest and began stroking her fears away.

But things were not as they were. She had withdrawn her hand from his genitals as though waiting for some reassurance.

27

"Gojorlovely," he whispered. This was not enough and she did not reply. He went on: "It's the best it's ever bin since I left home. I ran away from home when I was forty. I had a wife and children and a house with rooms upstairs. I used to be Father Christmas at Christmas. All that. I couldn't stand it. Everything seems over. First they're calling you dad, then grandad and then you've had it. Did you see *The Moon and Sixpence*? That was about that. He went to Paris ..."

None of this, although quite interesting, was succeeding in convincing Caroline that Dobbin was not a policeman. In fact it began to convince her that he was. That he was trying hard to cover up a slip. He had lowered his guard after sexual satisfaction. His guard, she was convinced, had to do with covering up his job. He would know that it would not matter to a girl who broke into houses and shit and played fountains in the kitchen whether or not he was married or had children. No, it was his job. A man who had to be constantly on his guard against running the alphabet into one lump of childlike phonetics would be self-conscious about being something lowly. Especially with a girl from Ox filled with impersonal pronouns. Fucking, Caroline Latimer had discovered, did not lower a man's inhibitions for more than the duration of the animal act. It occurred to her that he might be a commissionaire or even a lollypop man; though she was not certain whether the latter worked on Sundays. Probably not.

"What's your job, Caroline?" said Dobbin suddenly.

"What, me?" she said.

It was perfectly timed. He *was* a policeman.

"Oh, I'm afraid I'm a civil servant," she said. It was her experience that you could not tell even broadminded people that you were an Official Receiver's examiner in bankruptcy. Part of the law enforcement machine that took one's home away as a punishment for not keeping up—payments, paper-work, pretences. You could not easily explain about being a fugitive from Summerhill or rigidly liberal parents.

"Do you work in the courts?" asked Dobbin.

"Sometimes," she said.

Whatever his job was, learning about hers released him

utterly. He pulled his arm from under her shoulders to enable himself to roll on top of her. He kissed her savagely. He forced her legs open with one knee and then re-entered her body with savage though not painful force.

"Dobbin, careful!"

"Gorjalovely!"

During the prolonged violence of the next half an hour she had fleeting feelings that he was totally unaware of her presence as a person. A feeling of rape.

"You'll have to stop," she said, from time to time.

"Jusaminute," said Dobbin.

She became aware, finally, that he was unable to achieve his final orgasm, though his erection was still steel hard. Caroline Latimer helped her aggressor, whispering expert instructions, scratching her finger nails along his spine until at last he landed his ecstasy into the net of fulfilment. And when it was over he took his weight from her and tenderly held her face and kissed her romantically on her lips, like a receipt. They were exhausted and speechless and drenched with the sweat and juices of the occasion, filled with the spirit of having survived a dangerous and thrilling ordeal. But also saddened by the knowledge which destroys marriage, modifies all human relationship, the Columbus syndrome: that sublime discovery, as viewed from the highest tree, is unrepeatable. One would never fuck again as one has just fucked.

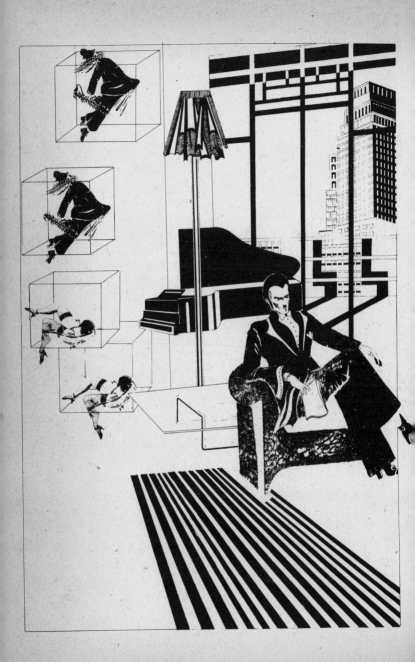

3

The dialogue between Caroline Latimer and Ben Dobbin was not finished. The physical act of making love conducted prematurely is like emptying the bowels before having eaten or even chosen the meal or done the cooking. The motion is perfectly satisfactory but one does not know what's in it. This was roughly Caroline's feeling. This and guilt. It had been an unusually super Saturday night but she had known two men practically within the hour. It was against her Catholic upbringing. It was against her Catholic fucking whore of a mother and her Catholic fucking vegetarian of a father. Freedom from religion was not one of the permitted freedoms at Summerhill. Instead of being everywhere, God was nowhere; for the healthy young atheist this meant long continuous searches. It went on forever. In the darkness of this strange room, it went on.

"One doesn't often do this," said Caroline Latimer. "And only at all since my engagement was broken off. That fucking bastard Warren Morgan and his bleeding dog. He was on the radio tonight. Last night, rather. Did you hear him? Dobbin? Dobbin? Dobbin!"

She managed to wake him up. He came around onto her swiftly, his organ still undiminished, his big hand clutching her nipple; she had to fight him off until he was awake.

"No. No, Dobbin. You can't. I've got a pad in anyway until it stops dribbling. You leave more than the milkman. Listen. I just wanted to tell you something." It had begun to occur to her that his continuing erection was unnatural.

"Wosermarrer?"

For Ben Dobbin, a simple uncomplicated man released into early middle age like a pit pony into green pasture, the night held no enigma, no guilt, nothing a good rub down and mucking out wouldn't take care of. He was, however, accustomed to girls like Caroline finding it necessary to explain what they were doing in his bed. Particularly if they had enjoyed themselves and particularly, it follows, since his affliction: the affliction which made a tent pole of the quilt if he lay on his back and could only comfortably be accomodated when he lay on his side with his knees up.

"One sometimes wonders if one has had all one's going to fucking have in this life," said Caroline Latimer. "I mean really. The mind boggles. At the end of it all one has, I should surmise, about six clearly remembered happy occasions. Then they wrap you away in your fucking shroud and put a short paragraph economically worded in the fucking *Times*."

"Wonnacuppatea?" said Dobbin.

"No thank you, Dobbin."

Her tone was kindly and thanked him for all he had done already. But it was also purposeful and wide awake. She did not want them to part in the morning and for this night to remain forever out of context. There was an American named Jim to whom she felt she had conveyed some of the tragedy of her personal life but knew from subsequent rather crude telephone calls that she had not. Some men were inclined to forget every blessed thing about a person except her cavities. And with some men, of course, it didn't matter. With some men—or boys, such were her tastes—it was purely masturbatory, nothing given, nothing asked. Raymond de Freitas was such a Hottentot, with his "fecking good riddance". There were people of both sexes you met at ex-patriate and political activist or Shelter or Amnesty International groups whose depth of intelligence you could echo-sound with the most banal remarks, the replies coming back like peas in a puddle. What one did was, one simply fucked them.

"We were both up at Ox, Warren and I." Caroline lay with her knees together, forestalling interruption. There was a curlicued plaster ceiling, which the street lights shone on, through the shutters. "I was in my second year, he was doing his Schools. We met at a party—Amy Farmer's. Isn't it odd, next week I'm going to have to take her house away on a bankruptcy order. One goes to university and learns how to destroy one another. Anyway; I don't think Warren noticed me very much. He went off with somebody else. But fortunately we had made this kind of date to go to a concert. So there was the party and then there was the concert and then we made love on the roof of his college—St Catherine's. After he had gone down he came up to Oxford to see me about three times and we slept together—twice in London. Then when I graduated he let me come and live in his house. He took this house in Hackney and this awful fucking mangy dog. It was all right for a time, but I couldn't stand the filth and the smell and I moved out. Then one weekend we got invited onto daddy's yacht. We sailed to Cherbourg, four of us in a thirty-foot sloop. I suppose that was the most heavenly weekend of my whole fucking life."

Caroline could not continue, but lay and cried silently in the darkness. Sometimes she could remember Warren as a distant dream, but then sometimes he was there in her senses like a hot flush, their feet touching in the pointed end of the little cabin. To her surprise she felt hot tears on her shoulder and found that Dobbin was also crying. She put an arm around him and gathered him in like a little boy. She thought it might be compassion for herself, or maybe it had to do with the Margery tattooed on his chest. It was a little of one and a little of the other, but mostly it was his incurable erection which he was gripping, like an enemy, like a cancer, with both hands under the sheets.

Warren's fatal flaw emerged at Cherbourg. We had had a rough crossing and Weenie in the aft cabin with her athlete perhaps rougher than anybody, yet she was shining. I thought you'd died. Did you, Mummy? A squint, no breasts, hair a disaster, yet she shone. Like an ugly town with God within it. That's what they called Newcastle, the Australian coal town, when I was in the Salvation Army as a child. It is not exclusively a lower working-class order as it is in Britain. I have been religious ever since I discovered that God is a word for when there is no other explanation.

34

Like any normal girl absolutely besotted, Caroline dangled her expectations from grandma's will into her lover's chest of goodies. Two astute lawmen together under each other's life jackets. Oh, darling, careful, yes, a most unusual case, darling—just a minute—oh, angel, wait for the big wave—yes, yes, yes, it must constitute a precedent, surely? With her sharp mind, soon after grandma's death, Caroline came up from Oxford and went to Somerset House to examine our marriage certificate. As she suspected she discovered that our family is founded on a spectacular and famous (within the family on two continents) runaway elopement to Gretna Green. We were not actually able, C.H. and I, to hit the anvil. Except at some local Scottish hostelry. You probably saw Wilfred Lawson as the leering host, calling up to the young couple in the old movie—it was just like that. "This isn't the Ritz, you know!"

The rest of my property, money, vehicles, buildings, investments, residues, clothes, jewellery, land and anything I might have forgotten, I leave to my son Charles Henry Latimer and his wife Isobel, but only so long as they remain married and together. In the event of a rift or their death the legacy goes in total to my two grandchildren, Julia and Caroline Latimer.

I will not go into our threshings after the will became known. The law is largely a matter of common sense and it is apparent that the old lady would have by-passed us had she known that we had fooled her all her life. C.H. got as far as the solicitor for the Writers' Guild in his dark office in Bouverie Street. My autistic daughter, I must put on record in this diary, offered to keep the secret from her sister in return for getting her share now. We decided to avoid this blackmail by making a family announcement. We are now voluntary trustees acting entirely for the beneficiaries. The autistic one now came out of the aft cabin.

"We've been talking about my investments, mummy. Daddy, tell Warren about my Australian Consolidated. He thinks he can unload them for me ..."

But it was not lucrative, this flaw; he was not a crook. A humorous young man with an Oxford flair and manner whose great-great-grandfather, he assured us, had been murdered fighting the slave traders—"For more money!" he would add. He also had his quota of modicums and boggles, a kind of academic patois, and a gift for understatement bred into the well-bred. He had a face like Rupert Brooke, long blonde hair and one earing, avoiding in his dress both the dated and the cool. He had known all the best people which endeared him for a time with C.H. The flaw was

35

undetectable yet, infuriatingly, you knew it was there. Warren Morgan is the piece of exquisite china you buy in a "seconds" shop; if anyone but Weenie had brought him home this simile would not have applied.

The flaw was exposed as it had to be, without confession or admission but as part of the unavoidable C'est la vie. Everybody's doing it now. Murder, it was, no less. Such a nice boy, hardened, one would suppose, by working on the law-surgery side of the profession, mixing with gutter criminals. After tying up and searching for chums in the small boat harbour, we had gone into Cherbourg for food. You may know how everybody from everywhere—that is Southampton, Salcombe, Dartmouth, Burnham-on-Crouch, Dungeness—heads for Sandy's Bar at Cherbourg. Partly nautical, some S.S. still, a small nucleus of geriatric English theatricals. Some French too, of course, unavoidably. Hamburgers and chips. No matter what the crossing was like you don't talk until you are stuffed. This gives C.H. time to present a civilised reason for not handing over our daughter's fortune to a new young man. The Oxford aplomb is enormous; but C.H. is Cambridge.

"I am at the moment changing accountants," he said. "Any transaction is out of the question until it's settled."

And thereby hangs a rather depressing tale, familiar to free-lances I expect. We have been with Jimmy Phillips the showbiz accountant in Davies Street for years, always dealing with André Joubert, as English as your old hat, of course. When C.H. discovered that he was fiddling us as well as the Inland Revenue on our behalf, he gave him the boot. At least, he tried to. Joubert threatened to shop C.H. for tax evasion unless he received a £7,000 golden handshake. C.H. who is superbly moral, who has, may I say, grown into his C.H. Latimer Exactly BBC crusader image picked up a telephone and asked for his MP. And after that there were terse letters and a quantity of steam at the end of which—when it had cleared, that is—Joubert was found to be still hanging tenaciously to his claim for £7,000. There is no doubt that we had benefited on the interest due on grandma's fortune, although the capital was not legally ours; this inescapable crime Joubert had manipulated as a lever against C.H., should it ever be needed.

"There's only one way out of that, sir," said Warren Morgan. We were now in a quayside bar full of wet people in yellow oilskins and drinking fit to bust. "Is there, Warren?" said Caroline; she was hanging on to one of his thighs still. Warren said: "Do you mind if we leave the ladies, sir?" Weenie and I went back to the boat.

Something terrible had happened. I could see that by C.H.'s face. Autistic people are swift to sense sea-changes; Weenie kept quiet apart from chatter. She wanted to catch the tide, get back in the aft cabin. This was not to be, however.

"I think I'll work topboard," Warren said. "If you don't mind sir."
"Shall you, Warren?" said Weenie.

C.H. and I were not able to talk until we shared the supper duty in the galley. I said: "What's happened, Charlie?" He said: "He offered to have him killed for me." "Who killed?" C.H. was trembling. "Joubert. André. He said for £2,000 he could get a contract out for him. All he had to do was pick up a phone!" I said: "That's a lot of money." Because at first the enormity of what is being said has no way of getting into the brain. Money has. "Our daughter has been sleeping with a man who can arrange murder. By picking up a phone. And he can actually tell me about it! C. H. Latimer. Exactly!" I said: "What are you going to do?"

C.H. went to the Law Society and also wrote to the Home Secretary. He had had him on his show and played his favourite records, the march from the opera Prophet and Gracie Fields. Within two months Warren Morgan had lost everything. Thrown out of his law firm, blacklisted, unemployed, living in squats in Hampstead. I saw a picture of him once when he was up on a drugs charge; sad indeed. But the truly resilient bounce highest when they hit the gutter and Warren Morgan struck fresh, heady altitudes of law surgery as the druggie's friend, squatter's advocate, champion of the under-privileged. Weenie followed him all the way down and part of the way up and nobody ever told her what had happened in Cherbourg. An autistic would not find a murderer remarkable company. When his decrepit old alsatian finally got her—not with its teeth but its smell—Caroline came home and cried for a whole week. It was the best thing that had ever happened to her. Autistic children cannot cry and when they do it marks an important change. Like the tin man in The Wizard of Oz, she had got her heart.

C.H. was shattered by this first glimpse of a decadent society (Warren Morgan) and this is what gives his BBC radio show its sincerity. The search for decency. People who believe in God move him enormously. Believe me, I do understand that, indeed I do! The values C.H. understands I can support him in, but without Caroline we should be cut off from the outside world. Caroline is now fireproof; she is our fire boat against the devil's armada. We know she carries a gun, she knows better than to use bad *language in front of her father. She is our knight in Harrods armour, the invincible, newly-emerged autistic, meeting old evils with a fresh eye and a clean sword. Nothing man-made can defeat her.*

"I have a lot of time for Caroline," says C.H.

We are the uncertified in a sick uncertifiable world. No white man's plague shall wipe us out.

Dobbin's dilemma would not have become a part of the dialogue but for the milk going sour and flocculating the morning tea. Caroline awakened to the clink of cups by the bedside and was in time to see Dobbin going out of the room, naked. It was not a clear image as her contact lenses were still in their little bath. Her watch by the bed said seven, and sunlight lay already hot in the room. The temperature would be 95°F by midday. People not old enough to remember the glorious summer of 1947 were getting frightened. There was a rumour that the earth had tilted on its axis.

"Dobbin. Dobbin! Is there any other milk?" Caroline called.

He called back from the kitchen without making an appearance. "Wossat?"

She repeated the question; her tea in its ubiquitous clay mug was swirling with specks of white.

"Yesacorse," he cried. And: "Jusaminute."

Caroline Latimer was not helpless. She went naked to the kitchen and interrupted Ben Dobbin at what appeared to be an attempt to piss in the sink. In fact he was trying to splash cold water onto his great stiff penis.

"Oh. Sorry."

"Sallright."

"Are you having a wash?"

"No. I've already had a barf." He struggled with his cock as though it had a life of its own, the cold water cascading over it. Caroline could see that he was in a state almost of panic. She came closer.

"Why doesn't it go down?"

"Dunno."

"I expect it's this hot weather. It was blown down last night."

He spared a puzzled glance.

She said: "When you found me here. When we met."

He shook his head and forelock pendulumed. "I had it stuck down with Sellotape," Dobbin explained.

While she thought about this unusual behaviour he gave up in despair, turned off the tap, padded his cock with a little green towel and then absentmindedly hung the towel over it as a convenient rack.

"With Sellotape?" she said.

"Dinwanna frighten you off. Give a wrong impression."

"Then you must have known I was here!"

"Corsadid."

"Then why were you naked at all? I mean, why go to the trouble of sticking yourself up with tape—why not put on some clothes?"

"Haven't got any clothes," said Dobbin.

"Haven't you, Dobbin?" Alarm chimed in Caroline's voice for the first time. Considering the events of the night in this strange house it said much for her equilibrium. For the first time also she remembered the gun in her handbag.

"I'll get the milk," she said, with artificial normality. Obviously Ben Dobbin did not live here at all. He had broken out of some lunatic asylum. That's why he had to get back in time for Sunday visitors.

"Where's the broom cupboard?" she asked. People who pretended they lived somewhere never knew where the broom cupboard was.

Dobbin was kicking the refrigerator; once, twice on the side, then a tug at the handle and it opened. He passed her a new pint of milk. "Wossat?" he said.

"It doesn't matter," said Caroline Latimer. If he knew the secret of the fridge then it was his home. Dobbin was now cupping two handfuls of ice cubes around his genitals, a sight that touched her deeply. She said: "Does it hurt?"

"If I'm not horny. Sort of aches. It's all right if I'm horny."

"Let's have some nice tea," said Caroline. She had no intention of engaging in therapeutic sex at seven in the morning. While he poured the tea and put in fresh milk she slipped on knickers and dress. They sat together on the bed listening to the morning news. There was an item about some dissident Russian writers which Caroline did not quite catch. It meant something however to Ben Dobbin, who gave his penis a smack, setting it waving.

"Thassoo started all this here. The Russkies."

"Did they, Dobbin?" said Caroline Latimer. She was more interested in finding some of his clothes than listening to his lunatic talk. It seemed absolutely true; there was no sign of a shred of clothing, not even shoes or boots, in either the kitchen or his room. There was only the pillow case with holes torn in for his legs. Two wardrobes appeared to have been cleared right out. She said: "How are you going to work if you've got nothing to wear, Dobbin?"

"They'll bring some. The boys. They take 'em away at night and bring 'em back in the morning. 'Cept when we're on nights. Then they take 'em away in the morning and bring 'em back at night. Is there any more tea?"

Caroline fixed him some more tea and some for herself and offered to cook him some breakfast, never letting her carefully casual questions appear the least bit important in case they were mistaken for an interrogation. She had learned that some people hit you if they thought they were being interrogated.

"And why do they do that, Dobbin? Take your clothes away?"

"So I can't go out, a-course. So I can't rape anybody else."

"I see. Did you—rape somebody, then?"

"Course I did. I raped dozens. I was always raping at first. Well, we all were. What would you do with this bloody thing sticking out in front of you all the time. It's insatiable. Has to be fed, dunnit? Crumpet, crumpet, crumpet, day and night, night and day. It's like stuffing buns up an elephant's trunk and coming back for more. Dunno what I'd a' done last night if you hadn't turned up. Margery had to go to Pete."

Caroline tried to keep up; she touched the name tattooed over his heart. "Is this she?"

"Yesacourse. I had that done when we clocked up a hundred."

"A hundred rapes?"

"Well, she gets paid. I mean, she's on duty. They share it, the WPCs with a few volunteer outsiders and a couple of pros."

Caroline said: "Do you mean Margery is in the police force?"

"Wellacourse. We all are. They couldn't use civilians on a job like this. Get out of hand. There's a dozen of us in our squad. Men, I mean."

"And have you all got this—complaint?" She almost touched it, but reconsidered in time.

"Six have and six haven't," said Dobbin. Then with a certain flush of crusading indignation, he said: "Thasswotamean. It's too neat, arf an' arf. That's what I said to Pete. They've been trying it out on us. You work it out. We've been picked according to circumstances." Caroline Latimer sat holding her teacup in its saucer and watching Dobbin tapping his knob onto the palm of his other hand to make his points. "There's two married, two single and two homos. That's not accidental, miss, mark my words. Somebody's keeping records. I notice Captain Turner hasn't got it."

Caroline said: "Are you telling me that somebody has *done* this to you?"

"That's my belief, miss."

"Don't keep calling me miss, Dobbin." It had been a very pleasant night; she was struggling to maintain a romantic relationship. "How would one *do* such a thing?"

"I'm not allowed to say, miss. Miss Caroline."

He suddenly sounded like a policeman and she connected this with his glances at the clock; it was nearly time for duty.

"Aren't you, Dobbin?" Guilelessly she had taken her hand from her cup and placed it on his penis, as if holding his hand. He swallowed tea and took a great gulp of air and spoke all in one infinitude.

"OmyGod!" And: "Phew!" As if he had received an unexpected electric shock. He suffered her hand to stay there; every moment it becoming more bearable. "Gothatslovely. You shouldn't, miss. No, don't move it. It was beginning to go numb. Ready for duty."

"I am sorry—" She removed her hand but he grabbed it and put it back.

"Too late now! We'll have to have another go or I'll never get through the day." He put down his cup on the bedside cupboard and rolled Caroline Latimer back onto the pillows. She pushed his arm away and squirmed off the bed.

"No Dobbin, I'm sorry. Not in the morning. I'm too relaxed. One keeps going and going and achieves nothing. Warren used to want me in the mornings—no, please!"

While she was talking he had manoeuvred himself into a position from which to grab her arm; his hand slid down to her wrist and he pulled it to his erection.

"Oldit! Oldit! Thassalliearsk! Godisawful! Ta. Thanks. Gobless."

"Now look. I'm sorry, Dobbin. I am not going to sit here holding your cock all day. I may have to go to Godalming."

"Give it a suck!"

"No! Fuck off, Dobbin! Piss off! Let me have my hand back. I shall scratch it! I warn you. I'll pull your fucking foreskin. I had to do that to Warren once. I can assure you it's jolly painful. I don't know why I sweated to go to Oxford, I've had nothing but humiliations. All those fucking spastic housewives when I was working for SOC. Accusing me of having it off with their cretin husbands. Girls who leave retarded schools and go to work in Woolworths don't know how well-off they are."

While Caroline was getting all this out of her system she was gently massaging Dobbin's stem, which is why he was not paying her particular attention. When she stopped he moved himself against her hand, trying to reach orgasm. She frustrated this, removing that hand in order to consult her wrist watch.

"What time are your friends due, Dobbin?"

"Not yet, miss. We shall be all right."

"I don't want to be all right, Dobbin. I'm sure Margery will oblige. In the line of duty. I just wish I had understood the situation a little more clearly when you were telling me how lovely I was last night. One likes a modicum of sincerity when one's giving one's all, so to speak."

She stopped speaking for a moment and when she spoke

again the sarcasm and bitterness had gone from her voice; she had noticed something about Dobbin's erection. She said: "It's turning blue!"

When Dobbin looked up at her, having first looked down at his penis, his eyes were filled with tears. Caroline was reminded of his compassion during the night when she had told him all about Warren and the cruise to Cherbourg.

He said: "It goes like this if I get passionate and don't do anything about it. Then it aches again."

"Can't you toss off, Dobbin?"

Dobbin looked out of the window. Caroline Latimer sighed her understanding. "Yes, of course you do. All this working-class guilt about it."

"I'm a policeman."

"You'd better let me hold it for a moment."

Ben Dobbin lay back against the pillows exhausted, pushed his pelvis forward for treatment.

Caroline put down her cup and shot her dress cuffs back, like a nurse, before going to work. She said as she worked: "Are you sure you won't tell me about it?"

"Gojorlovely, darling," murmured Dobbin.

"Yes, we know all about that, don't we, Dobbin."

She sat tailor-fashion on the bed, her bottom down between his legs, and stroked upwards from the root with all her fingers, like a potter throwing a pot. Sometimes she ran one hand down lightly under his scrotum, making him gasp and writhe. She had her contact lenses in now and appeared to become genuinely interested in what was happening, her face coming closer as the acorn came higher. When a little juice appeared from the eye she licked it off like a mother cat. This was too much for Dobbin. He reared up and grabbed Caroline and neatly reversed their positions on the bed.

"No, Dobbin!"

"I gotta! I gotta!"

He cleared all opposition and thrust into her, only to stop with a puzzled expression. "You got your knickers on."

"And they are staying on, Dobbin—until you tell me how it happened."

"Let me come in and I'll tell you. God's honour."

"Will you, Dobbin?"

"It's an official secret. You'll have to promise not to let it out."

"We are both members of the judiciary. One might say."

This seemed to settle the question: Dobbin ran his hand round underneath her bottom and she lifted herself in co-ordination and settled into a rhythm.

"Now?" said Caroline.

"What?"

"Whistle and ride," said Caroline Latimer, firmly.

With various passionate interpolations from Dobbin, Caroline Latimer heard for the first time, in a most apposite situation, about Operation Sycamore. In an indirect way it was also a further dialogue concerning her father, C. H. Latimer's well-known impotence. Caroline, at Summerhill as a girl, at St Anne's as an undergraduate, and in her professional life and amongst those groups and solitaries which constitute the blasted oaks, landscape features—fraught and friendly of her Green Line and BR social route through life, was known as a lady who never lived through one aimless moment. Behind that short-sighted crinoline exterior was a busy little factory working all out on Caroline Latimer priorities. What gave Police Constable Ben Dobbin the horn might very well give daddy the horn.

4

"Gojomarvellous ..."

"Slow down, Dobbin, whoa back, you promised, not so fast, you're hurting—there!"

With one dexterous movement at the cyclic moment of maximum withdrawal she sent Dobbin's cock boring into the bedclothes.

"Shit!" he said. "That hurt, miss."

"Did it, Dobbin? It serves you right. Once you come you'll never tell me. Why Sycamore?"

"Let me come in and I won't move."

"Why Sycamore?"

"Because it's a menace, miss. The seeds are dropping everywhere. Sycamore trees are springing up all over the country. And the towns. They've got their own aeroplanes, those little spinning things. Roads and pavements are bursting up. They grow five feet a year. That's like this drug. That's what we're fighting, miss. Can I come in now?"

"Oh, it's a drug, is it? Not yet, Dobbin."

"Just let me put it in the playground. I won't put it right in."

"Won't you, Dobbin? I wonder. For a new complaint it has a remarkably familiar prognosis. One more question and you can go on fucking. Is it animal, vegetable or mineral?"

"It's a vegetable, miss. Gojorlovely."

"And do you take it or inject it?"

"You said I could come in. Open your legs, miss."

"Oh, very well, Dobbin. Now—what kind of drug?"

"Omagod! Christ! Phew! Up! Up! Up! Wriggle and jump, miss! Like you did before!"

"I will not wriggle and jump until you tell me, Dobbin. Don't kiss me, you can't answer questions if you're kissing me. That's a typical male trick. Have you got any of this drug here in the house?"

"Yes! Gojourfuckingmarvellous!"

"Where is it? Where is it, Dobbin? I'll close my legs if you don't tell me—"

"In the vegetable bin! It's in the vegetable bin! It's a lettuce!"

Caroline Latimer tried to prevent the policeman's ejaculation, but she was too late and he collapsed onto her as though having completed the final stretch of the Grand National. She pushed him to one side and used her vaginal muscles to squeeze his unflagging pole out of her.

"You are a bleeding fucker, Dobbin," she said.

"Wosermarrer?"

"You know perfectly well wosermarrer, Dobbin. You tricked me. First you talk about sycamore trees and now it's lettuces. You've got nothing wrong with you at all. You're just a fucking stallion out to grass. One accepts anything rather than admit one's as randy as the next. Well, it's been very nice and I'll know where to come next time I'm on heat. If I was really vindictive, of course, I'd send mummy."

"Would she come?" Dobbin asked.

"You are the giddy limit, Dobbin. You really are."

"No disrespect, Miss Caroline. I s'pose I'm a bit crude. I never fucked a lady before."

"Haven't you, Dobbin?"

"You're not a barrister, are you miss?"

"I am an Official Receiver's examiner in bankruptcy, if you must know. We are now in the Thomas More building in the Royal Courts of Justice in the Strand. Now if you don't mind I am very uncomfortable. I want a shit and then a good hot bath. I'm sure my cunt must look like a whitewash bucket."

There were some people who were stunned by Caroline Latimer's choice of language. Now that Dobbin had managed to assuage the hunger of his hungry cock, he was stunned by it. He was also hurt that she had rejected his explanation. He got off her and at the same time managed to wrap his blue-and-red steaming barber pole in a bit of the sheet. Caroline sat up slowly, as though she had been on her back for twenty years and had just met Jesus. She groaned and lifted her arse and gradually got it off the bed.

"Youwallright?" asked the policeman.

"Comparatively."

She was not unhappy. It had been a super Saturday night, one of the best. There had been eighteen orgasms before she forgot to count. It ought to last her through the week. She could put her mind on her studying instead of on those pimply young men in court. Have a few coffees on Jimmy the Weazel and perhaps dinner with Timothy at Keats without even showing her knickers. Rams like Dobbin allowed one to be completely independent and liberated. Bachelor girls knew how to store up sexual satisfaction across innumerable deserts.

"Aren't you going to get ready for work, Dobbin?"

"I'll have a bath after you. I can't get dressed till they come for me. They're late. I expect they're getting the dogs." Caroline looked across the bed at him; she had one leg up and was wiping the worst off with tissues. Dobbin sensed her disbelief. "It's true, miss. Everything what I said. We use dogs to find the stuff."

"Do you, Dobbin? The lettuce, you mean. Vegetarian dogs, I take it."

Dobbin remained silent and Caroline went off to fix her bath. Miserably he looked after her and a tear ran down his cheek. Nobody believed it yet. They would though, one day, when it spread like a weed, all the men going round with three legs.

"Ben."

Where Caroline had just gone out, a policeman now stood; helmet in hand; a tough-looking man with a bruiser's nose but now diffident, as if talking in a public library or aware of intruding into a private occasion.

"Are you all right, mate?" he asked Dobbin.

Dobbin made signs that he was not alone and indicated a swift conclusion of their business. "Give us me clobber and wait outside, Nick."

Nick said, "Okeydoke", and slung a black cardboard laundry box into the room. Then he sniffed. "Blimey. Smells like a brothel. Hurry up and get dressed, the captain's here. He wants to come in with the dog."

Dobbin said: "Oh Christ. I 'aven't washed yet. Wait till she's gone, tell him."

Nick went out and came back with a considerate afterthought: "Will you be wanting Elsie for ten minutes?"

Dobbin indicated that he would not, and his colleague left.

When Caroline came from the bathroom carrying the clothes which she had found time to slosh through in the hand basin, Dobbin was in the kitchen standing on newspaper and giving himself a good wash down.

"Thorsavewaiting," he said.

"Did I hear voices?"

He was too busy to spare her a glance. "They're outside waitinforme. Got me clothes. Yallright?"

He was not waiting for replies and he did not therefore notice her staring at his penis, still hard and erect, running with Fairy Liquid soap.

"Anything less preposterous and I might begin to be convinced, Dobbin," she told him.

"What?"

"Are the dogs here?"

"Cominininaminute." Now he looked at her. "You better go, Miss. Don't mention the lettuce, will you? We're not supposed to have none."

"Then why have you got it, Dobbin?"

"Withdrawal symptoms." He was now standing tiptoe to engineer his tool under the running cold tap. "Makes it better for a little while but makes it worse in the long run. That's what Dr Jacobski says."

"Who?"

"Dr Jacobski. Jake, we call him. He was in right from the start. In Russia. When they were growing it for rabbits—listen. I think they're coming—"

"They can't come! I'm not dressed. I've got to iron my things. Where's the iron and ironing board?"

"Perhaps you'd better stay in the bathroom."

The police and the dogs could be heard mounting the stairs. Caroline Latimer was quite unflustered but annoyed.

"I will not hide in the bathroom, Dobbin. One does not spend a perfectly private night with a friend and then become subjected to invasion by the police force or dogs sniffing for fucking lettuce. All right, I've found it."

Caroline was pulling the ironing board out of a cupboard by the sink when Sycamore came in—three men, one woman and a dog. Besides the constable Nick, there was a thin bearded sergeant wearing his tall helmet, suitable for mobile caravan units though not for squad cars, the plain-clothes army officer, Captain Turner, and Elsie, a worn WPC. The dog was a black alsatian called Tiger, straining on a short lead held by Mick. They at first politely ignored Caroline because of her nakedness, but then after a moment when she seemed to be in danger of trapping one small breast in the ironing board, the sergeant tried to help her.

"Are you ready, Dobbin?" Turner asked. He was a big man of about fifty wearing young men's gear, black shiny jacket in leather, plain khaki-drill trousers with an old-fashioned taper down to his veldt suede boots. He was still wanted for murder by the Palestine forces. There was a port-wine birthmark over his right eye and temple. He had a public-school voice deep in the throat.

Dobbin obviously was not ready, and when he hurried out of the kitchen to dress Captain Turner looked at the naked girl, now spitting on her flat iron.

"Don't believe we've had the pleasure, miss?" he said.

"Piss off," Caroline Latimer said. Tiger was trying to get up to a plastic three-tier vegetable bin on a working surface under the kitchen window. The men went on regarding Caroline as she ironed her clean knickers. She stopped and looked at them, icily. "May one iron one's fucking knickers without a jury?"

Captain Andrew Turner smiled. "You've a damned good seat. Has anyone ever told you that? Hm?"

Caroline Latimer said: "When it comes to arses, captain, I should think you know more about the brigade of guards. Now fuck off or I'll put this hot iron in your other bleeding eye."

"He's after the marrers," Nick was saying about the dog. He was talking proudly to the bearded sergeant, Sainsbury, as the dog put its forepaws up on the working surface, whining for the big green marrow. "That's logical thinking, Trotters. Marrows are more like big cocks than lettuces are. Cut him a bit, Elsie, let him try."

She said: "No. They may not be Ben's. This is a shared flat. Get down dog. You're not very hygienic, Nick."

Undismayed, Captain Turner was standing closer to Caroline, recognising his own class: "Understand your feelings, of course. It's a damned imposition, all this, in peace time. But it is a state of emergency. Women are getting raped. We're off to Chelsea Hospital. You can't throw pensioners into prison. Best we can do at present is give them more gals. You're not on the rota, are you?" To his squad he said: "Stop mucking about. You won't find it there. Dobbin's not daft." And again to Caroline, officiously: "I have to ask you this, Miss. Have you seen any red lettuce on these premises? I must ask you to be truthful. It's in the national interest. Even one small leaf? Think."

Caroline had put on her pink knickers, but found the bra still damp. She lit two gas rings and hung the bra from the dish rack above by trapping the straps under a saucepan. She spoke to the Captain from these pre-occupations without very much interest. She felt that lettuce was probably a code or nick-name for something like hash or LSD. It was still inconceivable that a paramilitary special branch should be conducting a nationwide purge against salad. Chelsea pensioners were probably hardened criminals in the trendy pseudonymous slang.

"We probably ate it for supper, Captain."

Captain Turner took this in the spirit in which it was offered, rather than as information. He said: "I hope not, Miss. It might give Dobbin a bigger erection but it gives women beards. Doesn't it, Trotter? Trotter's a WPC, aren't you, Trotter. She was the belle of C Division until she started nibbling *cultivas rouge*—now she's a hairy-arsed copper. Aren't you, Trotter?"

"Do shut up, sir. Think of something new."

"Off you go now, men," said Captain Andrew Turner, in the kindly but firm manner one uses on dangerous special mission. "Search every room in the house. You've got the keys, Sainsbury? Good. I'll be cross-examining Dobbin. Elsie, stay and have a word with the lady." His glance at the WPC conveyed the nature of the word.

All went out and Caroline was left alone with the young policewoman. They folded up the ironing board together, dropping the heavy steel legs on each other's feet.

"Had a hard night, dear?" Elsie asked.

"I'd rather not discuss my personal life with the law."

"This is not official. I'm complaints officer. We don't want anyone unhappy. Talking to the papers. You're Caroline, aren't you? I'm Elsie Thompson. I often help Dobbin. We try to keep three or four regulars. Otherwise you start to feel like a tart. Dobbin's very nice but he can be demanding. Well, he's one of the worst cases. It broke up his home. He had a wife and three lovely children till this happened. There ought to be compensation."

Caroline began to feel that she had misjudged the situation. Her legal mind came up like carp after worms at the prospect of redress. An authority that had to rely on screwed girls not talking to the papers and injured policemen not suing for damages was in a very vulnerable and interesting situation. She adopted the quiet, friendly, engaging and rather complimentary tone of intelligent inquisition, which somehow reflected her own high opinion of her victims's intelligence. It was something quite subtle that she had learned from dealing with furtive bankrupts, dark with secrets. One also learned to betray no surprise, but rather to have some familiarity with the situation, no matter how alarming the disclosures. Here, almost immediately, was an example.

"After all," said Elsie, who had now composed herself comfortably on a kitchen chair, "his wife's family are all suing Dobbin. Why can't Dobbin sue the state?"

"Well, quite. How did Dobbin offend his in-laws?"

"Raping and screwing. You know what he's like now, sort of running down. When it started—that would be a year ago—he was rampant. He raped his wife's mother, screwed every female in the family over fifteen and put his wife in a wheelchair. You notice this house is empty now. It was full of girls when Dobbin moved in. There are something like sixty sexual assault cases pending."

"It will all come out in court, surely, Elsie?"

"What court? You must be joking, dear. The lettuce is sub rosa." She pressed down on the kitchen table as if kneading dough. "You know—kept under, suppressed. Until the back-room boys come up with something."

"What are they looking for?" Caroline asked.

"I don't know. A weed killer. That's what it is, isn't it? Mind you, my dad thinks it's an act of God. A plant that was bred to multiply rabbits. That's man being God, isn't it? Instead wipes out the human race."

"Rabbits?" said Caroline.

"I think your bra's scorching, dear," said Elsie.

What she really thought at that moment was that she was talking too much. Caught offguard by what appeared on the face of it to be an anomaly, that anything as stiff as Dobbin's cock could possibly wipe out the human race, rather than do the opposite with a population explosion, Caroline had betrayed her ignorance of the basic root element in this obscure national emergency. In her scheming mind she was grasping at straws of information that might turn into the kind of profitable haystack she could take to Warren Morgan and his crusading legal eagles. She put her bra on back to front in order to fasten it, then slipped it round and squeezed her boobs comfortable, at the same time giving the young policewoman a reassuring smile, which however, in certain lights with contact lenses, looked a little shifty.

"I'll fetch your dress for you, dear."

"And my shoes," Caroline called as the girl went out. "I think they're somewhere in the bed."

The policewoman laughed back at her, understanding perfectly. As both women were aware, the small errand was only an excuse for a short conference with her superiors and with Dobbin. In the quick time she was gone Caroline managed to search the vegetable bin without finding a lettuce either green or red. In the middle of this the police dog Tiger rushed in and shoved its nose up her bottom, the constable Nick following and pulling it off and apologising and wrestling it out of the room. Now Elsie came back smiling, her caginess gone. She had had good news about Caroline Latimer.

"So you work in the High Courts?"

"Yes, Elsie."

"Well, that's lovely. I tell you what I think you ought to do, dear." She sat down at the kitchen table again and rummaged amongst the scraps left from somebody's last meal. "Have you got any cheese? I'm starving. It makes you eat, doesn't it? My dad said you're fucking all night and eating all day. Mind you, it's often the other way round—ta, dear." Caroline had found the policewoman some old Stilton and a bit of rusty celery; Elsie now went on enthusiastically with her mouth full: "This is what you should do. Join the rota. Getcha name down, dear. The pay's good. All they ask is you sign a little form. Only a little one. To safeguard themselves. Twelve pounds fifty a night. That's not bad, is it?"

Caroline said: "Not bad at all, Elsie, if you happen to want to be a fucking prostitute. Where are my fucking clothes?"

"Didn't I bring them?"

"I gottem." A policeman had come into the kitchen holding Caroline's dress and shoes. It took her a moment to recognise Dobbin in his uniform. Now she understood the poetry of their instant rapport. He had been so familiar, she thought she might have met him in some previous life. Now she knew where it was—on point duty up at Whitestone Pond. Every rush hour he and his colleagues were landmarks, standing at the highest point in London, the same height, give or take a few feet, as the top of the spire of St Paul's cathedral. She looked to see if she could see his affliction, but if that lump was it then it was hardly discernible.

He gave her his faithful horse smile. "Yallright?"

"I don't know, Dobbin. Ask Elsie. I don't know whether I've just been insulted or recruited."

"Everybody fit?" The Captain had appeared with Trotter

behind him, Nick and Tiger sniffing around the doorway like bloodhounds waiting for the trail. "Come on, Elsie. Bring that grub with you." Captain Turner then looked brightly at Caroline: "Are you likely to be here later in the day, miss? Say about noon? I've got a couple of the boys will be in a pretty bad way by that time—"

He broke off, rather too late, because the young policewoman was making cancellation signs behind Caroline's back. Caroline's head came out of her dress, the rest of her naked still, apart from the panties; her face was quite pink.

"I beg your pardon, captain?" she said.

He took a pace away from her. "Scrub it. I'm sorry. I thought perhaps you had decided to join our rota—"

"You pimp!" said Caroline. "Do you honestly believe an Oxford BA is going to screw at your prices? I wonder sometimes why I wasted my fucking energies. O-levels, A-levels, crammers. You end up teaching idiots or fucking policemen."

"Put your dress on, darling," said Dobbin.

"Don't call me darling. Don't let your captain think that anything about last night was normal. Please get out of here and let me finish dressing in peace."

Dobbin hung back for a last entreating word: "Shall I see you again, Caroline?"

"I should think it's rather doubtful, Dobbin, wouldn't you?"

"I thought perhaps I might take you out to tea or something? The pictures, perhaps? You could come and see my mum in Stevenage."

She softened toward him but would not yield. "I think I know what you're trying to say, Dobbin. Thank you."

Dobbin was trying to say that he could do ordinary things with her. That he did not regard her as a hole for this terrible machine. The others had drifted out into the hall as a diffident gesture toward the lovers' goodbye. She touched him gently on his bulge and said, softly: "Just take care of this."

He said: "Couldn't you leave your telephone number somewhere?"

"No, Dobbin."

Police Constable Ben Dobbin then did a curious thing for a policeman. He took Caroline Latimer in his arms and kissed her, at the same time whispering into her small ear: "Put it inside the marrow!"

"Come along, Dobbin!"

"Coming, sir!"

He looked round at her once as he went out of the kitchen; she dropped her long dress down to her feet as though it was a curtain on the whole affair. But when she was quite certain they had all gone she got the big green marrow in which Tiger had displayed so much interest and inside, where the pips are supposed to be, she found the red lettuce.

5

It was Sunday morning of that same rather super weekend. Caroline Latimer was now in what she termed an up-beat mood. One had to strike while one's luck was running. Having dressed herself and pulled the bed together and made a few gestures towards washing up and tidying debris, spraying aerosol to mask the general decadence, she used Dobbin's telephone to make a call and save herself possibly fourpence.

"Timothy?"

"He's not here, I'm afraid. Can I take a message? He's at a meeting of the bishops."

"Is that you, Martin? This is Caroline Latimer. How are you keeping? How's your leg?"

"Oh, much better thank you, Catherine. They wanted me to have it off but I wouldn't. There are so many worse things happening in the world. Did you read about that woman and her little boy squashed by a reversing milk trolley? They're electric. I've always thought them too quiet. There's another coach crash. The police have killed some football fans—of course I could see that coming."

"The mind boggles," said Caroline. "What bishops, Martin?"

"I'm not quite sure. There's a lot of hooliganism going on for the archbishop's throne. The Roman Catholics are ganging up on the new boys."

"Timothy's not a Roman Catholic, Martin."

"No, I know. He's only driving. He's taken Father Leary to Bermondsey in his Morris Minor. He tried to ring you. Have you been out? He's taking the boat down to Godalming to see his mother. How did the funeral go?"

She registered that Martin had got her confused with somebody else. One would expect it of Martin Pushkin, an elderly blonde queen mother, his house full of antique furniture he ran bits-and-pieces stalls—and half-and-half men; Father Leary in the attic now God, Timothy working his way up from the basement. Catherine must be another of Timothy's girls he fed at Keats. Caroline hoped the funeral was of somebody close. Taking her silence for grief, he went on:

"Don't weep for the dead, petal. They're better off. The next ten years are going to see complete and utter anarchy. A person won't be able to go out shopping and leave his home unguarded. I'm telling you, sweetie. The meek will inherit the gutter. That Nazi is still in my second-floor front. Ranting and roaring and breaking his girlfriend's arms. She won't go to the police. We daren't use the kitchen except when he's asleep. He thinks I'm Churchill. I didn't even like Churchill. I can't get him out. We've all been to law. There is no law, duckie. That's what it's come to. Have a nice day on the river. Isn't it hot again?"

"Martin," said Caroline.

"Hello? Yes?" He seemed surprised to find somebody on the other end of his complaints against life.

"Do you know if Timothy's taken his swimming things?"

"He took a towel. He couldn't find his trunks. He can swim in his Y-fronts. Try to make him eat something, Catherine. He's not cut out to be ascetic, living on gruel and the Ten Commandments. May I be perfectly frank? Timothy needs a woman."

"I'll pack a nice salad," said Caroline, managing to look exceedingly like a witch as she said it.

"Put a bit of sand in his petrol, sweetie. Tie up somewhere for the night. Bideybye."

"Bideybye, Martin," said Caroline.

"Do it before that awful cross-eyed graduate lady from the bankruptcy courts gets her talons into him," said Martin Pushkin.

"Capitalist prick," said Caroline Latimer, keeping the receiver to her face after the line had gone dead.

There were very few things one did with one's weekends if one was a graduate working in London. Zoologists would go to the London Zoo or out to Whipsnade; a Green Line to Dunstable and then a bus. If one was a politician or journalist in one of the economic or social areas one scanned the *New Statesman* for lectures and demos. Arty people found concerts, galleries, discos, pub·theatre. The BBC issued lots of tickets these days and now one could also lie in bed and phone in on commercial radio, joining issue without commitments or personal confrontations. It was all what Caroline Latimer called Durex Land; wherever university graduates rubbed together in their post-graduate lives there were Durex ads. Behind every desperate advertisement "Genteel lady wishes to meet opera lover"—was the need to stop babies. If you failed to stop them your BA with honours took you no farther than the kitchen sink. Medics fucked and had parties and played moronic games.

Now back in her own room in Highgate and naked except for a flowered straw picnic hat, Caroline ran her Parker 55 down the pages of her Boots desk diary. Soon she would carry out the rest of her witch's transformation for enchanting Timothy, but first she had to find out more about the magic potion. The names and addresses and telephone numbers on these shiny quarto faint-lined pages were the fruits of one's university education. Somewhere here there had to be a field research person, a botanist, agricultural scientist, plant biologist. Yes! Where was Fran? Fuck. Fran was in Canada. She should have done her phoning from Dobbin's. Here was a possibility. Elliot Frazer; Elliot was with Fisons with his science degree. A biological insecticide expert. Caroline dialled Bar Hill, Cambridge.

"Hello. Is that Mrs Frazer? Is Mr Frazer there, please? This is Caroline Latimer. I believe we met at a May Ball?"

"Oh yes? How are you? He's in the garden. Can you hold on?"

While Caroline Latimer was waiting at her telephone in Highgate for a man she had met perhaps three times at Oxford, five—no, six years ago—she began to unwrap from its Snappie covering the red lettuce she had stolen from out of the middle of PC Benjamin Dobbin's green marrow. She began, to be accurate, to try to regard it as a serious problem that had suddenly arisen in the middle of a Sunday morning. By the time the scientist had arrived at the phone she was ready for him.

"Mr Frazer? Elliot? I don't know whether you remember me. I wouldn't bother you if it wasn't rather serious. At least, it might be. I need some expert advice."

"Caroline Latimer?"

"St Anne's. We were at the Lit. Soc. My father came and lectured. C. H. Latimer of the *Mail*?"

"Good lor yes. Vegetable man. Rather my line. How are you, Caroline? Nice to hear from you. You must come and see us. What are you doing these days? Law, wasn't it?" "Yes. Fancy you remembering. I'm in the High Courts."

"But how terrifying."

"Not really, Elliot. I help people. With their financial problems. Bankruptcy, in point of fact."

There was the short embarrassed hiatus with which the word bankruptcy is invariably greeted by the respectable non-bankrupt world. This is followed by a jolly laugh usually. Elliot Frazer gave a jolly laugh.

"There but for the grace of God, eh? Ha ha ha. What can I do for you, Caroline? It's not money or the law, I hope? I'm in insecticides. Natural ones, that is. Using nature's own poisons. It's a fascinating field."

"One of my clients claims to have grown a red lettuce," said Caroline Latimer. She was holding it in her hand now, a beautiful object; long and fat and soft, cos-shaped. But the beautiful red-veined leaves, moist and close, were crimped in a ring around the top, giving the whole lovely vegetable an unmistakeable likness to the male sex organ, though something like four times normal size.

"Can you repeat that, Caroline? A red what?"

"A red lettuce."

"There is no such thing as a red lettuce, Caroline."

"That's what I thought."

"He probably means a cabbage. An ordinary common-or-garden pickling cabbage. What shape is it?"

"It's lettuce-shaped. Like a cos lettuce. Long and firm and with a kind of—ahem—well, thing at the end. Acorn."

"Really? Have you seen it?"

"What? Oh, no. Not the actual thing itself. I've seen a picture of it. A colour print. Yes, that's right. You see, he's been sending out a prospectus. Inviting investment. That's why he's in court. He claims all kinds of incredible effects for it. Medicinal, you know."

"Rubbish. The man's a fraud. A quack. There is no such thing as a red lettuce, Caroline."

"Not even in Russia, Elliot?"

"Is that a joke?"

"Oh no. He says they were bred in Russia."

"I see."

Caroline Latimer began to get the feeling that she had rung the wrong person; or that he had changed since Ox. She said: "Well, thank you, Elliot. Sorry to have bothered you. It does sound rather ridiculous in cold blood."

"What's this fellow's name?" the scientist asked.

She detected a shade too late that he had no interest whatever in the fellow's name; he was trying to catch her out. He thought she had rung him up because she was hard up for a man. He had probably just remembered what she looked like.

Caroline gave him the name of a genuine fraud; the one who was about to cause the sudden death by suicide, very probably of Amy Farmer, the Barnum-and-Bailey swindler she would be facing once more in the Thomas More building on Tuesday morning. "Maurice Bernard Rayner."

"Is he a professor? The name rings a bell. Of course he could be mad. A lot of them are mad."

"He's a promoter, Elliot. A business promoter. He's the man behind Anex. Those green crystals for dog lovers."

"Green crystals for dog lovers? Just a minute, darling—I have to get the runner beans in. No, I don't think I've ever heard of that, either."

"Oh, I see. Well, they are on the market, Elliot. When your

dog fouls the pavement you just sprinkle them on. Antifoul. Everybody's buying it. He ought to be a millionaire. I musn't keep you. Thank you, Elliot.''

"Listen, Caroline. Don't go." Either his wife had moved out of earshot or the mention of Anex had cast doubt on his reliability as an expert; if he had never heard of Antifoul it was quite possible that he had never heard of red lettuce. In the world of science, once you were over thirty and going bald, you only needed one or two blind spots to start rumours. Soon one discovered that only unimportant experiments were being delegated to one, the answers, very often, already known.

"Yes, Elliot?"

"If anything does come up," he said, unknowingly apposite, "I'd really be most frightfully pleased if you'd fill me in."

"What about, Elliot?" She merely wanted to hear him put into words what a moment ago did not exist in his mind.

"The—er—red lettuce."

"Yes, of course, Elliot. And if you get hold of it you can fill me in."

"Rather ..."

Caroline Latimer sat there for a moment, rubbing the red lettuce reflectively. Used cleverly and with a bit of careful planning, Dobbin's red lettuce could give an awful cross-eyed graduate lady considerable powers. She could not easily forgive that fucking old queer his remark, and several times as she clothed her body to suit the straw sun hat for the river, she posed in front of her full-length mirror; sometimes twirling her blank and flowered Japanese sunshade, sometimes catching up the hem of her long blue chiffon skirt and a handful of white layered petticoat as one would when stepping into Timothy's little Micro-Plus cruiser. With one's eyes half closed one could look very beautiful.

Soon Caroline Latimer began to prepare the picnic salad. It was now eleven. Timothy would not leave Port Hampton on Platt's Eyot until two o'clock, because that was when the *Rising Sun* shut on a Sunday afternoon.

6

To reach that part of the Thames out on the Lower Sunbury road from Hampton Court, travelling from Highgate in north London without a car, takes a stoic London Transport expert. One walks down Highgate Hill to the Archway station, carrying one's wicker-work picnic basket and parasol and handbag. One then very cleverly books only to Cannonbury, four stops, and takes another short street walk to the BR north London station from which one can circle straight round to Richmond via Kew Gardens. From Richmond a bus to Sunbury puts one down at the great water-reservoirs, from where a short walk brings one to the concrete bridge by the river police harbour and thus to Port Hampton. By the time one has walked across the long bridge and down the other side and then round through the boat yard and along the mooring path one's arms are being dragged from their sockets.

But the boat, Merrymaker, is still there, for it is not yet turning-out time, and Caroline has time to prepare for sailing. It is a quarter-hour job to remove the canvas hood from the cockpit, connect up petrol and calor gas and steering, wash the dead flies from the superstructure and give the sleeping cabin the woman's touch. She had remembered to bring a litre bottle of Timothy's favourite wine, red Hirondelle. Timothy, slightly pissed, arriving at quarter-past two, had brought with him Catherine Vesey, Lady Kate, that is, reputedly Bonny's current girl friend, thrice denied by the palace and therefore Fleet Street's most serious contender for a future lightweight Lady of England. A pretty, blonde, fag-smoking plumpish girl in force-faded blue denims. Her father was the Duke of Waterlow, squire of a hundred thousand acres in Hampshire and Lanarkshire. In the absence of eunuchs she was allowed out with men like Timothy. Or at least, so one supposed, if, like Caroline Latimer, one was trying to wipe the last of the fudgy black grease from around the outboard motor when one saw the laughing couple walking towards one, hands linked.

"Fuck!" she said.

"Fuck!" said Lady Kate at about the same time.

"Oh Hell," said Timothy. He sounded like the late Edward Everett Horton playing the deprecating butler. "Dear me. Well well. What the devil is she doing here?"

"Ahoy there!" cried Caroline.

"Ahoy there!" cried the pair.

"I was just going," lied Caroline Latimer. Besides the book of possibly useful contacts, Oxford and Summerhill, plus C. H. Latimer as a father and Isobel Latimer as a kind of mother, together with her own brain factory behind her sly contact lenses and with the additional power of potent red lettuce, Caroline also had the facility for swift contingency thinking. As quick as a click of the thumb she had seen, in the appearance of Timothy and Catherine, the beginnings of an interesting social experiment. She had no wish to create Dobbins in any haphazard manner. The incurable stiff prick could reorient the post-graduate world. Even alter monarchic history.

"We met at the *Radio Times* mid-summer party," Caroline called to the shore. "My sister, Julia Latimer, is an assistant producer at the new BBC Manchester studio—you wrote her up."

"Caroline and I were at Oxford," Timothy told Catherine Vesey.

"Come aboard and have some wine," cried Caroline. "And then I'll leave you to it. Elliot Frazer's picking me up. Steady now. Let me hold your hand, Catherine."

Timothy brought the girl aboard his little motor cruiser. He understood nothing. Catherine thought she understood something. Caroline understood everything. The bottle was opened, the wine poured; they sat around the bench seats in the small cockpit, smiling with the afternoon, brushing away the flies that came from the heavy willows, half-waving to passing boats. "Cheers!" they said. And when Timothy met Caroline's eyes above the rim of her glass, she said: "I telephoned Martin."

"Ah. Yes. Quite. I see. Yes, indeed."

Yes, indeed. Martin explained nearly everything. Martin, whose job was cooking eggs, thought that Timothy had been trying to ring *Caroline* when really he had been trying to ring *Catherine*; had finally found her at sauna with an empty Sunday. Caroline had brought a picnic and her sun hat and parasol and chiffon for the river and was now graciously backing out on a few believable lies.

"Martin said you hadn't packed anything. I've brought you a nice salad."

Catherine Vesey said: "How very nice of you. Are your sure? Why don't you come?"

"Mummy's expecting me in Guildford. A Masonic dinner or something. Next time, perhaps, if the summer holds up. How far are you going?"

Timothy said "Not far" at the same time that Catherine Vesey was saying "Godalming". To an experienced river voyager like Caroline Latimer, this constituted a contradiction. There were seventeen locks on the Wey between Weybridge and Godalming; two more before one reached the Wey. Most of the locks were unattended and would take, depending on traffic, half an hour each to negotiate. In the Micro-Plus with its 4 h.p. outboard, Catherine and Timothy drinking Hirondelle and the red lettuce salad as an unknown quantity, Caroline would reckon on two days sailing with two nights moored. They would probably get back to Platt's Eyot about Tuesday midday. From this one might assume that Timothy had at last decided to lose his virginity. As a consort of bishops it would have to occur with a member of the aristocracy.

"We could drop you off at Guildford," said Catherine. "We should be there by tea time."

"Tea time when?" said Caroline.

"Let's have some more wine," Timothy said. "Then we ought to cast off." For his sixteen-foot cruiser he was wearing his yachting squadron cap with badge and a pair of khaki Bermuda shorts with a pair of blue denim deck plimsols. With his lantern jaw and religious eyes he looked, Caroline now thought, like a fucking bank recruitment poster. "Goodbye," she said. "I'll look out for you at *The Jolly Farmer*."

Catherine was untying the tiller from the bow end of the line.

"No no, darling—" Timothy was helping Caroline ashore—"not that end. Lines tie up on the shore. You need them again. Cast us off, Caroline. Thanks for the tuck. Did you check fuel?"

"There's half." Caroline unhitched both lines and pushed the prow away from the grass with her foot. Timothy started the engine at first pull and grabbed for the gear.

"We're going backwards!" cried Catherine.

"Always cast off and moor against the current," said Timothy, giving lessons. "You have more control. Same with aircraft into the wind."

Caroline called across the widening water: "Don't forget to sun the bedding!"

Catherine Vesey's face came out of the cabin and looked at her with the refined beginnings of alarm.

In later years, as part of her Hailsham lecture at Sussex University on The Caucasian Erection, Caroline Latimer would include the happenings that day on Platt's Eyot as being catalytic to her involvement. It was also very nearly the last day of her life. Having seen Timothy's little launch puttering down towards the fuel pumps, Caroline had first gone to the marina toilets to make herself comfortable and get some of the engine grease from her hands. After this she strolled around the chandlery store to see if there were any men worth picking up. There were not. Catherine Vesey, surprisingly, was buying chocolate and cigarettes. She smiled rather nervously at Caroline.

"I saw you come in here. Timothy's getting petrol. Is he all right? I've only been with him at parties and so on. Don't know him frightfully well. Two chocolate flakes, please, and twenty Rothmans. And a box of matches. You wouldn't change your mind and come with us, would you? I want to strip off."

"Timothy's perfectly safe," said Caroline.

"Well that's what I thought. Oh, thanks very much. I'm afraid I've only got a five-pound note. That's what Honoria said. She slept with him and he didn't do anything. Very gentlemanly. He asked her and she said no and he went to sleep. Only since you went he keeps giving me funny looks. Then when I look at him he suddenly remembers to smile."

"It's because you're titled. He's a fucking awful snob."

"Oh! I never thought of that. That's all right then. You didn't mind me asking, did you? I hope I didn't mess it up for you, Caroline. I do remember your sister. I didn't like her."

"Nor do I," said Caroline.

They parted on the wooden steps of the shop.

"See you at *The Jolly Farmer*, perhaps," said Caroline. "It's a lovely beachy kind of bend in the river just beyond Guildford You can swim there."

"Fabulous," said Catherine Vesey. "Let's say eight o' clock."

This time Caroline Latimer watched the Merrymaker revers into the stream from the floating fuel dock and head aroun the island. By walking back through the boat yard and past th security hut, she was able to stand on the ramp of the bridg and wait for Timothy and Catherine to pass underneath. It too some time and soon she saw why. Timothy was lettin Catherine Vesey take the helm. The little white cruiser wa spinning from side to side, narrowly missing moored craft. On could hear Lady Catherine's shrieks of laughter and terror she over-steered, first one way and then the other.

"Cunt," said the experienced Caroline Latimer. She ha rowed at Oxford and at Henley in fours and eights.

It was then, while climbing higher towards the bridge plank that Caroline noticed the man.

"That is to say, if one can be said to have 'noticed' Mou Everest" was how Caroline Latimer described this first sight Norman Drake, during her lecture. This is not to say th Norman was a big man, but that in the life of an Oxfo graduate swimming the featureless pond of the seventies a chained to the concrete of her learning, Norman was a r and an island. She did not know this at first sight, but she the chemistry. A feeling, be it admitted, for which she was always instant. And in his strange and mysterious behaviour lay the first intrigue. Had he not been, clearly, a watcher, rather than a looker, Caroline Latimer would have passed on and caught the bus to Sunbury.

"I felt certain, as one would, bearing in mind recent circumstances, that this man on the bridge had some connection with *this*!" And on the word Caroline would bring the big sharp carving knife down on the board to chop another thin slice from the red lettuce. There was a gasp from the audience, for the scarlet veins of the tight-packed leaves had the cross-section—irresistibly—of a hard cock. The vegetable was more generally known, by this time, as the rabbits' revenge. Behind her back, as she travelled the university circuits, Caroline Latimer was known as the mad cock-cutter.

But this is dipping into the still uncertain future. She was wrong on one count. The intriguing stranger at that point in time had no connection with Sycamore.

7

Norman Drake was a hot man on a hot day in a hot place, then. This summer, although a late starter, was the hottest, sunniest summer in the entire history of recorded weather. Heat is a man's province. The hot waterless parched weeks would not be apparent, the temperature and the humidity and that need for air, the wet and smell of sweat under armpits would not so easily be evoked in the daily toing and froing of Caroline Latimer and other frilled citizens in the bus queues and tube platforms and marbled corridors of the Royal Courts of Justice. On the river the girls and the children and the fat women in their bikinis and regatta dresses shot the heat with the cool of colour, of breeze and bunting and long cold draughts of laughter. Hot man stood on the bridge, supported by his grimy elbows, and watched.

As Timothy's cabin cruiser snaked its playful curly route under the bridge and at last the captain took his rightful place and headed her for the open channel beyond the island, the man on the bridge took out a white handkerchief and before mopping his forehead waved it vertically, once, twice, thrice.

"Funny," said Caroline Latimer, to herself.

And then, at first unconnected, but soon more apparent, a police launch with engine already idling in the police harbour below the bridge, started out in quiet pursuit of the marked boat. Caroline, half-way up the foot ramp, turned round and hurried back onto the island.

"Sycamore. Fucking Sycamore."

She had the feeling (erroneous as it turned out) that this man was one of them. That his hard penis was probably strapped securely to his waist. For the first time since Dobbin told her that he had no clothes, Caroline Latimer again felt fear. Felt that she was the only private citizen who knew about the red lettuce. Felt that she had been followed all the way from Highgate. Felt that the man on the bridge imagined—since he must have watched her cleaning the wretched little cockleshell—that she was now aboard and taking the horn to Godalming. All of these feelings, or feltings, were inaccurate. They came through the human tendency to see the universe through the porthole of one's own current predicament.

"Miss. I say, Miss! Missy! Oy! Phew! This ain't no day for running. Not when you got one o' these in front of you." The security man had left his hut and run after Caroline as she hurried back toward the boat yard. Hearing him coming she had started running, and such were her preoccupations that when he spoke of having 'one of these' in front of him and patting his belly, she thought he was patting an incurable erection. She began to feel that she would never be normal again; would never be able to converse naturally with the opposite sex. This was a fat man in a brown suit wearing some kind of peaked cap of authority. Usually, coming and going to and from Platt's Eyot, one could just see the top of his head. He was there to justify the mooring fees, to keep the island inviolate from thief and vandal: those, that is, silly enough to come from the mainland and stagger back across the long footbridge over the police harbour with their nicked engines and dinghies, instead of merely—as happened frequently—slashing the mooring lines and towing them down to fifty thieves' boatyards at Kingston, Richmond and Teddington.

"What do you want?" Caroline asked.

"Nothing, miss. I thought perhaps you was looking for something? Somebody? If I can be of any assistance?" He looked her up and down; he had already noticed her leg silhouette as she climbed the bridge. "There's a loo in my place if you want to go?"

"No, thank you, I've just pissed," said Caroline Latimer.

The security guard's face was drained of all colour. Only men pissed and only men talked about having pissed.

"I see." He touched his cap as a reminder to her and to himself that he was on duty. He said: "Do you have a boat moored on this island, madam?"

"My friend does. He's just gone orf." Caroline Latimer was capable of throwing the middle-class-educated book at officials when necessary and 'orf' was a a part of it. She added, lying: "I'm waiting for him to come back."

"Would you mind stepping into my office, madam, and signing the register?"

"I've never had to do it before."

"There's royalty on the island today, madam. This chap's a policeman coming now. Excuse me! Officer! Can you spare a moment, sir?"

Norman Drake spared a moment. He nodded to the security man: "What is it, Sam?" And then he smiled at Caroline. "Went without you, did they?" he said.

Caroline laughed and said they did.

"Well, two's a crowd on a boat that size," said Norman Drake. "Though I expect they'll manage."

Caroline said: "Why are they being followed?"

"Security. We always follow Katy. I've been following Katy since she reached puberty. She's only allowed out with debs' delights, but there's always the risk of a bomb or a kidnapping. Is that your brother? Timothy Whatsit?"

"No. Just a friend."

"He's safe, isn't he? Not a mad raver or anything? We can't have Lady Kate getting preggers. That's what it's all about. She can't go on the pill. Some women can't. Do you want a cup of tea?"

"I would love a cup of tea." Caroline looked at Sam the security man, who looked as though he felt that he had become redundant. "I'll sign your register and you can check my handbag for bombs."

"Very well, madam. Thank you, madam."

They returned into the long security hut.

"It's hot," said Norman Drake. "It's very hot."

"It is hot," said Caroline Latimer.

"It's going to get hotter," said Sam.

While Sam in his brown suit was searching for a biro that had not dried up or was not exuding sticky ink, Caroline Latimer and Norman Drake smiled at each other. She was feeling fragilely pretty in her long flowered chiffon, see-throughable, and Norman Drake seemed full of good humour, although hot. He had an Irish, potatoey sort of blunt face, hair and eyes brown, ears a bit too big. He wore dark-green flared slacks and sandals with no socks and a very white T-shirt with "Alcatraz" in a crescent across the chest. Caroline felt that she had caught a butterfly; not a rare one, but one she had not got.

"There you are, miss," said the security man.

"Don't forget your telephone number," said Norman Drake.

She gave him a smile of mock reproof. She was surprising herself. One would have thought one had had enough policemen for one weekend. She did the necessary signing and she displayed the contents of her handbag, which were observed briefly and delicately by both men. She had brought enough pads to provide comfort and protection against several Dobbins. That this gave an erroneous impression she could tell from the shadow of disappointment in the new man's face. She was pleased to see it, guessing his expectations:

"Tea where?" asked Caroline Latimer, brightly.

She stood up from the old varnished rosewood chair, waiting to be escorted somewhere exciting. The wood boards of the shed, uncovered, swept but never washed, walked by boots and shoes from the river paths, gave out puffs of dust between the cracks with each footfall.

"On my boat," said Norman Drake. "It's an ordinary twenty-foot Dolphin. I need a pretty girl."

Caroline sat down again. "Why?"

"It gives me civilian cover. It's a Q-boat. There's some drink aboard."

Caroline bucked up. "I suppose you couldn't take me to Guildford?"

Norman Drake was not sure. "I have to go wherever Katy goes."

"They're going to Godalming. Timothy's mother lives at Godalming. Is that bad?"

The young policeman had sat down and covered his hot face with his hot hands.

"Godalming, miss?" said Sam, in a tone that explained the general depression. "Are you sure?"

"Yes. I'm afraid so."

He said: "I'll put the kettle on, Mr Drake."

Norman Drake uncovered his face. "No, Sam. Thanks." And then he said "Godalming." And then he got up. And then the window of the security shed smashed with the noise of metal hitting glass and Sam's face was suddenly covered in blood. Or so it seemed to Caroline Latimer. The interval of time allowed for shock is somewhat shorter in the presence of a man trained and waiting for just this occurrence. Even so it took a second bullet to explain the first. This one clanged on a new-looking free-standing electric radiator. Norman Drake tried to pull Caroline off her chair.

"Get down on the floor and stay here."

She resisted him. "I will not. Stop it. Leave me alone. That floor is filthy."

Instead he pulled her away from the desk and held her behind him to one side of the smashed window. He said: "Are you all right, Sam?"

Sam said: "I don't know, sir. Is my ear on? I think I've got a bit of glass. I'm all numb—" Sam stopped talking as a third shot hit the wall outside. Norman was trying to get a view through the dirty window without exposing his head. He said: "Dial 999 and say Royal—give 'em location."

While the security man appeared to be doing this Caroline was relieved to see Norman Drake take a gun from somewhere inside the top of his trousers. Holding her close just now, she had assumed the lump was part of him; that he was one of them. Sam said:

"The line's been cut, Mr Drake."

"Listen!" said Norman. "There's somebody round the back." He crept to the door as if to meet whoever was moving through the rosebay willow herb at the back of the shed. "Don't move," he told Caroline.

Caroline moved. She went across to the desk and picked up

her handbag and took out her gun; nobody had noticed it in the search, once the Tampax had appeared. She went back to the window and holding the gun by the barrel she smashed out the remaining glass as she had seen people do in films. At the door now, Norman looked round at the noise and was in time to see Caroline Latimer take aim and fire. There was a sharp cry outside.

"I think I got one of them," she said.

"Where did you get that gun?" asked the policeman.

"It's my gun. I bought it." Caroline resumed her aim toward the bridge ramp. "I get into some jolly tight spots." She shot twice more towards the bridge. Norman Drake put his gun out of the door and sent a shot both ways, then sprang outside and spun half a circle with the gun levelled, returning in reverse motion to shoot into an elder bush. Caroline appeared at the door.

"Don't come out," he said. "They think you're Catherine Vesey. It's probably the Irish. They're as thick as two bricks."

Caroline said: "I want to see if I shot anybody."

"You'll go to prison if you did," he said, unable to look away from possible dangers. He seemed irritated that somebody he was supposed to be guarding—though she was not his official charge—had guarded themselves.

It made her cross. "What is one supposed to do if some fucking bleeding arsehole starts trying to kill one?"

Norman Drake was so shocked by her language that he put his gun in his trousers and came back into the threshold.

"I beg your pardon?" he said.

He looked so furious that it frightened her. She said: "It was self-defence."

"I'm not talking about that. I'm talking about your language."

Here was a man who struck her as very twitchweed, as Summerhill and Oxford people describe their roots. Her language was more important to him than the danger of a bullet in his back. She said: "You'd better come in or you'll get shot."

He came in, but he was disgruntled and accused her of trying to change the subject. Sam the security man appeared to be bleeding to death, though fully conscious and active, holding up an electric kettle as a mirror to his head. The blood now was dripping down onto the striped collar and brown suit.

"Where are you hit?" Norman asked.

"I don't know, sir. I don't know where it's coming from. It must have been a bit of broken glass."

"I'll bathe your face," Caroline offered. "Have you got any running water?"

Sam took her into a grimy little timber scullery, full of gangrenous pipes and shit-brown porcelain. "There's some toilet paper there, miss."

She said: "Sit on the lavatory and put your head over the basin."

Norman Drake, who had been scouting out of the windows, now looked in on them. "Keep your gun handy," he told Caroline. "I'm going for help."

"Can you get me a Mars bar?" she asked.

"You stop swearing." Norman pointed a warning finger at her as a parting condition. And went.

"Both my ears are there," said Sam. Like a child he had his head in the dirty hand basin and turned sideways, the blood now dripping into a plug hole filled with hairs and phlegm. Caroline Latimer regarded the job for a moment, distastefully.

"Have you got any Vim?"

"Won't that smart?" he asked.

"Not for you," she said. "For this filthy basin—just a minute." She had noticed something odd about the man's head, now that his uniform cap was off. "Do you wear a wig?"

"No, miss," said Sam.

She said: "Then you've been fucking well scalped."

There was an edge of glass just protruding from his hairline, but covered in a continuous weir of blood. He groped up towards it but she stopped him.

"Don't touch it."

"I'll bleed to death!"

"No, you won't. You must have seen cowboys and Indians.

One does not bleed to death. One is scalped. Come back in the other room. I'll try to stop the bleeding."

Her coolness, like the coolness of most professional nurses, in the face of mortal injury, came not from expertise but from a complete lack of interest whether the patient lived or died. While she had him sat back at his desk, washing away some of the blood and binding the severed scalp, glass included, with her underslip, soaked and wrung out in cold water, she related similar ordeals she had suffered at the hands of Warren Morgan, the solicitor. She explained who he fucking well was and then went on from there.

"One of his favourite tricks when he was drunk or wanted me out of the house or I had kicked his fucking dog was to try to cut my fucking throat."

"Who fired those shots, miss? Who's out there?"

"He would attack me with the carving knife, but first he would sharpen it on the steel, like a butcher does. Satirising the heat of his emotion, playing to the jury, sending up the courtroom-fucking-thespians at the Wig and Pen."

"How bad is it, miss?"

"How bad is what?"

"My scalp. Can you see my brain?"

"No, of course not. It doesn't sound as though you've got any brain. Your brain is not under your scalp, it's under your skull, Sam. It's going to be perfectly all right. They'll stitch it up, I expect."

"Do you think you hit him, miss?"

"Yes. I never miss."

"Did you see him, miss?"

"I don't know. Don't keep talking. One sees something move and one fires. Another thing he used to do was leave his passport out. As though accidentally. Mental torture. He wanted me to suspect he was secretly planning to go abroad. Take one of his druggie popsies. He specialised in handling all these little heroin whores. He kept getting the pox and couldn't screw for about three months."

"I think I can hear him coming back, miss."

"Wait here," said Caroline Latimer, unnecessarily. She took

up a stance between the open door and the broken window, covering her field of vision with the gun held at arm's length. What's that chap's name again?"

"Who, miss? Norman? Sergeant Drake. No, I tell a lie. Oh, Christ, my head. It's running down in me eyes again. It's not me brains, is it, miss? I don't half feel funny. Detective Inspector Drake. He was promoted after the princess was nearly kidnapped."

"Did he save her?"

"He helped catch the bloke. They broke both his arms in the police van. He's good with the royalty, is Norman. You're not royalty, are you, miss?"

"Only in Guildford," said Caroline Latimer.

"Drop your gun and don't move!" Norman Drake's arm and gun and head could be seen through the open lavatory window; the door had been left open.

"Piss off," said Caroline. Then she said: "Did you get my Mars bar?"

Detective Inspector Drake said: "Not while you use language like that. Is there anybody there I can't see?"

"Only me, sir," said Sam, from out of sight of the loo.

Norman walked round the security shed and in at the door. To the security guard he said: "Ambulance here in five minutes. You're not dying, are you?"

"I don't know, sir."

Caroline said: "He's got a pane of window glass under his scalp."

"We're going to have to leave him," said the policeman. "I want you to come with me, Caroline. On the Dolphin. Quick as you can."

"I'm in a filthy mess."

"There's water in the galley. We have to hurry. Your friends are up at Sunbury lock. That shot of yours may cost Catherine Vesey her life—they'll think you're a police woman now."

"You don't know what you're fucking talking about," said Caroline Latimer. And at his anger: "I do not propose to alter my fucking character for you or anybody else. One likes to retain a modicum of individuality. You go up the river. I am staying with Sam until the ambulance gets here."

"Thank you, miss," said Sam.

"Don't thank me. I want a fucking lift. My mother is expecting me in Guildford."

"I'll take you to Guildford," said Norman Drake.

"No, thank you, Inspector."

"Then I shall be forced to arrest you under the firearms act."

"You shit."

This young man had a waggish look in his eyes, waiting for her to say something else so that he could cap it. She liked him, but didn't know how to get aboard his fucking boat without losing face. "Have you eaten?" he asked her. She said: "Not yet." He said: "You took a picnic basket aboard your friend's boat." Caroline said "That was for my friends." He said: "You weren't expecting the other girl." It was not a question and therefore she did not answer it. He said: "There's plenty of food aboard. Duck. Do you like duck? Plus all the trimmings. A few bottles in the cold box. You can sunbathe on deck. We should be in Guildford by seven."

"Not if you follow Timothy."

This observation was a mistake on Caroline's part. She saw Norman Drake's eyes come on duty. She had been referring to the red lettuce in the salad, ticking away like nemesis. She knew already, what this Buckingham-Palace-oriented copper obviously did not know, that the pane of glass under Sam's scalp had been put there by Sycamore; that the bullets had been intended for her. That, moreover, when she failed to sign Elsie's rota for special duties, that is, relieving stiff pricks, she had put her life in jeopardy. Either that, or they had discovered the loss of Dobbin's red lettuce. She had been followed, she had been seen to make her contacts, she had been marked down as a red lettuce pusher, promoting the national horn.

"Why do you say that?" asked Norman Drake.

"Why *did* I say that, do you mean? If you say why *do* I say that, or why *does* one say this or that or the other what you're really asking is, why does one *always* say such and such, which is a nonsense."

Instead of side-tracking the young plain-clothes officer her hair-splitting rigmarole only confirmed whatever suspicion had come into his mind; he came closer to her, preparing to hit her for God and the queen. Caroline Latimer knew all the signs of forthcoming violence and moved away, concerning herself with the wounded guard. He appeared to have died.

"Sam, Sam!" said Caroline. "I think he's dead." She touched his arm, the sleeve of the brown jacket now stiff with blood.

Sam's eyes opened, the whites showing up in his bloodied face like the eyes of a nigger minstrel. He said: "Water."

She said: "Yes, of course. You poor thing. They won't be long. Let me get him some water." This latter, because Norman Drake seemed to be blocking her path to the scullery.

He said: "What did you leave in that basket?"

"A picnic salad."

"It was a bomb, wasn't it? What time is it due to explode? You'll tell me or I'll break your arms."

"Don't you dare touch me!"

He lunged to grab her and she sprang away, crying: "I won't be hit! I won't be hit! That's why I carry this gun." It was now pointing at him. "If you hit me I'll kill you. That's what I've decided to do to anybody who hits me again."

"Water. Water, miss."

"All right, Sam."

"Who are you?" Norman Drake asked.

"That's better," she said. "Now let me get Sam a drink."

He watched her go into the scullery and listened to the rising cascade of water notes in the mug and was full of indecision.

Caroline came back with the water in one hand and her gun in the other, but wanted to put it down while she helped the scalped man. "Pax?" she said. Norman nodded and she put down her gun and tipped the mug to Sam's mouth. And she said, without looking round from her task, "I have nothing against the royal family, I can tell you that. I am an officer of the royal courts of justice. I do not put bombs in salads." This was not absolutely true, was it?

"What makes you so certain your friend Timothy won't get to Guildford by seven?" While Norman Drake was asking this question he was seriously considering picking up her gun. She could read this in his potato face and sloshed the last drop of water down Sam's neck in order to repossess the firearm. Instead of pointing it at anybody this time she put it back into her handbag. Accepting this as a placating gesture, Norman slipped his hand up his T-shirt and brought out a Mars bar and gave it to her. She unwrapped it and took a genteel bite. It was warm and sticky and beginning to melt. She offered it to both men, as a politeness, then spoke with her mouth full.

"Timothy is a ditherer. You saw the way they were twirling around when they went under the bridge. He does everything at about two knots."

They smiled at each other as this conjured up certain images. Sam groaned and they stopped smiling.

"We could lie him flat on the floor," Caroline suggested. "He oughtn't to be sitting up like that. He's lost a lot of blood and he's in a state of shock. I expect they'll give him a general anaesthetic. They'll put you to sleep, Sam. Don't worry. When you wake up it will all be better."

"Yes, miss."

Norman Drake listened to this; she was making a good impression on him again. He said: "Are you coming with me?"

"Say Caroline."

"Are you coming with me, Caroline?"

"If you want me to, Norman."

"We ought to hurry."

"I'm not leaving this man alone."

"No," said Norman Drake. "Nor am I."

She was looking for somewhere to wipe her chocolatey fingers and Norman pulled a big white handkerchief from his trousers pocket. As he did so a solitary french letter which he had just scrounged from the boat chandlery store fell to the floor and lay there for a finite time.

"You've dropped a stamp," she said.

He picked it up and she wiped her fingers and thanked him. This tiny revealing incident fed itself into the devious processes of her private factory and by the time they heard the ambulance bell approaching the river on the far side, Caroline Latimer was already in full production.

"Now listen," said the policeman. "When the ambulance men come in I want you to stand over there with your hand inside your bag on your gun. You can shoot through the bag if necessary."

"Shoot the ambulance men?" said Caroline curiously.

"Oh Christ!" said Sam. "Oh God. Don't do that, sir."

"You don't let me finish," said Norman Drake. "The people we're dealing with in the royalty business stop at nothing. As they say. I mean, think about it. What a beautiful con trick. You shoot anybody except the person you want to kidnap. Then you move in with an ambulance, wipe out security and get the princess— or whoever— away in the ambulance. Chloroformed, most probably. All right, here they come. Are you ready?"

They could hear somebody approaching from the footbridge.

"You did phone for an ambulance, didn't you?" Caroline whispered.

"Shush!" he said.

A woman's voice was heard and then a man's. As they passed the man was saying: "If you really loved me you wouldn't say that." "But I do say it," said the woman. "You take everything the wrong way. Don't you? Don't you? Well, don't you?" The man said: "Have you got the rowlocks?" And then they couldn't hear any more and in a moment there was a loud clattering on the side of the shed.

"Anybody there?"

A little fat noisy man came in, carrying the stretcher which he had just bumped the length of the shed. Caroline had very nearly pulled the trigger and it made her furious. "Do you have to make so much fucking noise, you little fat squirt? It's enough to make one jump out of one's fucking skin."

"That's enough of that!" said Norman.

Two more people came in, a young woman in a green summer cotton dress carrying a doctor's case and a girl wearing an ambulance service hat with various hippy leather clothes. She was saying to the other woman: "That was a shocking case. I had to put my hand down the lavatory pan to get the foetus—

well, you've got to take everything back. Oh Christ—what's happened to you, soldier?"

"Just a minute," said Norman. "Will you identify yourselves please? I am Detective Inspector Drake."

"Didn't you send for us?" asked the ambulance girl.

"Yes. But I have to be certain of everybody in a situation like this."

"I am Dr Sandilove," said the girl in the green dress. "I have no identification—I was playing tennis. We've got equipment in the ambulance for blood transfusion and there's oxygen. How do you feel, Mr—what is your name?"

"Mr Rowley," said Sam.

"How do you feel, Mr Rowley?"

"I'm all right, thank you, I can't feel anything."

Caroline said: "He's got a bit of glass under his scalp. I don't think it's safe to take it out."

Dr Sandilove went to Sam and examined the wound very closely.

Norman Drake said: "Where did you qualify, doctor?"

"Edinburgh. Why?"

"Just checking."

"Get this man out to the ambulance." She had taken Sam's pulse, looked into his eyes, given him a reassuring handclasp.

To Caroline, she said: "Is that your slip on his head? You'll get it back through the hospital laundry. We're going to Sunbury General—come along if you like. What happened, Inspector?"

"I'm not allowed to say," said Norman. "You understand."

"Yes, of course."

"I wonder who I shot?" Caroline murmured.

Dr Sandilove turned from her supervision of the patient to look at Caroline for a moment. She said: "Are you next of kin?"

Caroline shook her head. The girl said: "We shall need his address. Mr Rowley, where do you live?"

"I'll take it down, doctor," said the ambulance man. "When we get in the ambulance."

"Camberwell," Sam kept saying, as they took him out on the stretcher, nobody listening.

"They seemed genuine enough," Norman Drake said, when they'd gone.

Rather reluctantly, Caroline thought. She suspected that he would have preferred a shoot-up. She suspected that like a lot of policemen he lived a very quiet life and was ready to explode any tiny occurrence into a 3-act drama, backed by the majesty of the law. One would hardly die of excitement following the Lady Catherine Vesey unless one occasionally caught up with her. An interesting possibility.

"Coming?" said Norman Drake.

They went out into the heat of Platt's Eyot and down the concrete path to the marina, the young inspector's hand gently holding her waist, the french letter in his pocket.

8

We are coming up to lettuce-testing time. Will C. H. Latimer's daughter find a dialogue bearing on her father's shortcoming? The mushroom that shrunk Alice so that she could go down a rabbit hole was no more astonishingly magic than the red lettuce from Trans-Caucasia, grown for rabbits, which had precipitated, that is hurtled and swept, this Official Receiver's examiner in bankruptcy into this super weekend.

"If you don't have a bikini you'll be all right in pants and bra," said Norman Drake.

You complacent bugger, she thought. He really thought he was going to get his leg over, no trouble, pad or no pad. The solitary french letter was to keep his knob clean, not on her behalf. Well, too bad. Caroline Latimer had already planned an alternative future for him. And not only an immediate future, either, such were her production plans when it came to the search for a husband. There were two sorts of men in Caroline Latimer's experience; or, that is, two sorts of salt one put on their tail to catch them. With one kind one had to be pregnant and unwilling to abort. And with the other kind, and this was Detective Inspector Norman Drake's kind unless she was mistaken, one had to be a virgin.

As they passed the chandlery store the owner called out to Norman, "Aye Aye!". And he put his thumb up and smirked at Caroline as if at the success of the Mars bar and the good use ahead for the french letter.

"Good afternoon," said Norman, suffused with guilt.

"Arseholes," said Caroline.

"What?" said Norman. And then: "Of course you can sleep aboard if anything happens and we don't make it to Guildford by dark."

She said: "I have to be at mummy's by evening or there's no point in going. I'm back in the high court in the morning. Ten o'clock sharp."

"Oh? I thought you were joking about the courts. Are you a typist? Secretary, rather." He was not actually interested and she did not actually answer him. She was a body in which to stick his prick; that was the extent of his interest. "Here we are," he said then.

The Dolphin, a cabin cruiser with a blue awning, the hull in cream, the cabin in light blue, lay moored two boats out. They had to step across a luxurious catamaran and then a rather scruffy converted lifeboat. He had stopped holding her—or feeling her would be more accurate; his next words explained why.

"We are on a television screen at HQ," he said. "Once we get aboard I'll swivel the camera forrard."

In a moment, crossing from one boat to another she lost her balance and clung to him, feeling the hard butt of his gun against her belly.

"Sorry about that," she said. This instead of "Shit" or "Fuck".

Norman Drake gave a helpless, sheepish duty-ridden glance at the camera. You would have supposed Caroline Latimer did not notice this particular fruit of her impishness because she had suddenly caught sight of Raymond de Freitas (fecking good riddance). He was at the bow end of the converted lifeboat, naked but for black swimming trunks and wearing sun glasses and apparently engrossed in splicing a rope or something equally ridiculous. It was this that had caught her attention— that particular turned-away angle of the head when the eyes can follow something without being observed. As Norman caught her and brought her down into the cockpit of his boat, below camera range, he held her closely to him. She was waiting for him to say, "Gojorlovely!"

"Sorry about that," he said, in waggish revenge.

She was looking past his shoulder. She said: "Follow that man into the lavatory."

Norman looked round and ashore. A man was going into the lavatory by the chandler's shop.

"He's got a bandaged arm," Caroline pointed out. "Hurry."

Norman Drake hurried back across the two boats onto the quay and ran towards the lavatories. Before he had reached them the man Caroline felt certain was Raymond de Freitas also hurried ashore and also headed for the lavatories. Caroline Latimer, still holding her large bag, also hurried ashore and towards the lavatories. The television camera on the roof of the Dolphin cabin watched all this. Or so it seemed. Caroline went into the shop.

"May I have a Mars bar?" she asked. The owner, or manager, Nigel Fury—silk shirt, cravat, white slacks and rope shoes, fair, unctuous, over-friendly—got her a Mars bar. "Pleasure. Must keep your strength up. It's a nice day for it!"

"How would you know?" Caroline asked. She gave him the right money. "I shouldn't think you've fucked anything since the menopause."

He watched her go out of the shop, watched her legs through the filmy long skirt without a slip, framed in the doorway, put his hand on his balls. "Filthy little cow!" he murmured. "It's the last time she comes in here." Then he grew interested in her behaviour outside the shop. He wandered over and hid behind a hanging rubber dinghy to get a better look. "Amphibious little prostitute!" he muttered. The middle-class girl from Summerhill and Ox had gone into the Men's.

"Oh, I'm sorry!" she said to the three peeing men. And then to get a better look: "I'm in the wrong place. So sorry."

She walked back in the sunshine to the quayside.

The man with the bandaged arm was pissing at least a foot higher than Norman and Raymond de Freitas ...

"Vaccinations," said Norman when he came back aboard.

"What?"

"That chap you noticed. The one with the bandaged arm. He owns this cat we're moored to. They're off to the Cape Verde Islands."

Caroline needed time to work that out. She was tidying the craft for the second time this Sunday afternoon. "Are these your knickers?" she asked then.

The Inspector glanced into the untidy cabin. A much bigger area than Timothy's little Micro-Plus and therefore more scope for mess. He laughed: "Oh dear. Sorry about that, Miss Latimer. I expect one of the sergeants left them there. The boys have been on a boat larceny down at Kingston. Well, and the girls."

Caroline just raised her short-sighted face to him. Momentarily. Like saying I've read about them: stripping, pornography, blue film clubs. Then she dropped the dainty garment into a maple-wood wardrobe. They were probably Catherine Vesey's. She returned the conversation to what concerned her more. "And what about the other chap?" The two men could now be seen standing by the chandlery shop and talking together. Conspiring. "He was aboard that converted lifeboat. Not the catamaran."

"Forget it. Nothing sinister. We help each other fit out. They've got nothing to do with those shots." Norman was preparing to untie. He suddenly chuckled, audibly, then grinned when she peered out at him. He said: "Annie get your gun. What did you say to poor old Fry?"

"Who?"

"Nigel Fry. Chap in the shop. What did you tell him? He's really spare. You're the limit, you are. I'm starting the engine. Leave that mess for now. Get ready to untie at the bow."

Caroline Latimer performed her nautical duties efficiently. Padding around the deck, balancing over the side, untying, preparing to cast off, talking as well, hitting at flies. Bloody Nigel Frys. They think women exist to lie on their backs and push Hoovers.

"What are you muttering about?"

She came back and cast off astern. They moved out into the Thames. The first water-born moment. Solidity gone. Smooth, liquid, unconnected, directionless. They exchanged a contented smile. She said: "I'll get the fenders in."

"Take that dress off. You'll be falling overboard."

"Soon, skipper." One had to navigate with extreme caution if one hoped to make a reasonable port. Her plan to be a virgin might work. When she absently unbuttoned the front of her chiffon dress, Norman Drake's throat visibly rose and fell. He now had her catalogued as a river nymph. She had known it was the mens' lavatory and she had entered and taken a good old peep.

"Comfortable?" called the captain to his crew.

"Mmmmm," said Caroline Latimer.

The Official Receiver's examiner lay with her bra undone and seen to be undone. She lay on her front on the hot cabin top, her face sideways on her hands and also underneath her was somebody's orange-and-black striped bath towel that smelled, an inch from her nose, of sour sweat. Her naked body was slightly across the keel line, her bottom in its little pink panties and her legs open enough to catch the sun and to intersect with Norman Drake's eyeline of the river ahead.

"Hungry, Caroline?"

She managed to convey a negative by wriggling her arse. A passing canoist saw this and caught a duck with one end of his paddle. "Fuck!" he said. She barely noticed him. She was worried about Tim and the lettuce somewhere up ahead. Sunbury lock came up and she went to her duties watched by the watchers on the shore. The fenders, the queue, sorting sizes, entering the basin.

"Up you go, love," said the man with the potato face.

"Aye aye," said Caroline Latimer.

Other pretty naked ladies went about their ship-to-shore duties like little celluloid dolls on an obstacle course. Back to the deck, holding lines, slipping them as the basin adjusted levels, heavily preoccupied. She knew what the lettuce did to Dobbins. What did it do to bishop addicts? Action astern took her attention: the catamaran coming up fast to make the lock. Too fast; a harbour authority launch peeped angrily and moved to intercept.

"Norman," she said. And then when he looked at her, she said: "Isn't it hot." Better not mention pursuit. Somewhere in the chugging hours ahead, Sycamore might be needed. She was still uncertain about this Inspector of river police. In order to steady her while she took in the slack, Norman Drake's hand and what appeared to be a gun butt had practically assaulted her, crutch and nipple. He smiled at her.

"So sorry."

"Are you, Norman?" One of her oblique expressions. As she said, "Did you, Mr Stowbrass?" when her bankrupts explained how they lost five thou on a horse when in fact they had hidden assets in Japan. It was an apparent gullibility which put even shrewd men in prison once she had encouraged then to sign their lies on oath—encouraged Norman's invested optimism in a french letter.

"I hate these weirs," said the captain, nervously. They had left the lock and the craft had separated out and now the Dolphin was forced to run close to a weir chain in order to avoid the yellow oil-skinned dinghies of the Middle Thames Yacht Club. He said: "I'm always afraid the engine is going to choose this moment to pack up."

"I'll open the wine," said Caroline.

Frozen in the memory, it was the third hot Sunday in July. Behind them, low on a treed horizon, the Goodyear airship hung, unreal as a holiday poster.

"Nice?"

Norman talking about the wine. She smiled her contentment. He was standing and steering and drinking. She perched on the gun'l. One was inclined to drink wine by the tumblerful on picnics, like lemonade. Until it overtook one.

He leaned across and wiped a splash off her right thigh and said: "I thought we might tie up to eat."

"Good idea."

"I know a quiet place on the Wey. The River Wey, that is."

"Do you, Norman?"

"We can swim."

"Super." The river way of getting her knickers off. Since she had nothing else to swim in and he knew it. A brisk rub down in the cabin afterwards.

"Cox's Lock."

Lots of cock at Cox's Lock, she thought. One could moor out of sight under the willows. She said: "What about the others?"

"What others? Who's that? Another drop in here, please Caroline."

"What about Katy and the assassins?"

"Oh! Ah. Well, we're getting shore reports, you know. I'll tune in to HQ soon. That red light comes on if they want me in a hurry."

Liar. The whole apparatus was switched off. He knew it and she knew it. His sexual apparatus was switched on and that was all. The drama in the security shed had been peripheral to her see-through dress and his freshly acquired french letter. The shooting was possibly nothing else than a bit of lucky vandalism. Unlucky for Sam.

"That canoist keeps passing us, Norman."

"No, he doesn't. It's not the same one. They're our chaps. Canoists are usually policemen. Open 'nother bottle. Stay there. I'll do it. Take wheel."

"Gosh!"

Quite suddenly Caroline Latimer had sole control of the boat. The last time she had been at the helm was taking the yacht into Cherbourg harbour. Different now, trying to line up trees and river traffic and cut approaching washes at the optimum angle.

"Lookout!" The frightened man's voice came from so close that she thought for a moment somebody had come aboard; she had in fact cut up a little cruiser on which two children were sitting way up front, their feet dangling into the water. She very nearly squashed them.

"Terribly sorry!" she called back, doing a kind of watery broadside and leaving them bobbing in her wake.

Norman Drake appeared in the companionway, tucking his cock out of sight, zipping up. "Sorry," he said, "I was peeing. What was that? I thought we'd hit something."

"It's perfectly all right." Caroline felt herself turning quite crimson. The end bubble of a french letter was trapped in his flies. The over-confident sod was getting ready. One of those chaps who lost his erection if he couldn't pop it in instantly. The chances were now that there was a hole in the bloody thing. Cunt. "It was that family behind us in the lock basin."

The policeman had vanished to get himself sorted out. Caroline looked back down the river, gave a friendly wave and was relieved to get one back from the little family man. She wanted as many friends as possible this afternoon. Little did she know it, but the family she had so nearly drowned were a part of the drama that still lay ahead. One mile behind, the catamaran trailed its steady pursuit.

9

He watched her spider her way across the deck as they came up to the lock mooring. Norman Drake made a promise to himself. He was going to get it in. What Caroline Latimer was thinking, as she dropped the gay-coloured plastic sacks down the side of the boat, was that he had finally abandoned all pretence that they were following Timothy and Catherine. He was quite ready to sail straight on up the Thames and spend the night at Runnymede after getting her helplessly pissed at the Angler's Rest. Pissed or not it was going to be a fight. He had tremendous strength. She had her gun.

"Get ready!" he called.

She balanced herself up at the bow as he brought the craft neatly towards the mooring piles, cut the engine at the right moment and did a short reversing burst to bring them in close enough for her to hold on and make fast.

"Good girl," he said. "I'll do this one. We've probably got a ten-minute wait. Lot of traffic coming down. They've only just opened the top gate."

A young bearded man in blue swimming trunks called to him from a motor-sailer coming in behind them. "Shall we get through all right, sir?"

Norman looked at the boat. "What are you drawing?"

The young man said: "About two feet, I think."

Norman said: "I'd go and see the man. He can let some more water in for you. Don't forget the more water the less the headroom for the bridge. Is that as low as you can get your mast?"

"Petey, no!" called the young man's girl friend. "I told you not to buy this one. Let's go up to Staines."

"Just shut up, Jenny," said Petey. "Who's captain?"

They moored and the young man jumped ashore and set off to find the man. Jenny smiled at Norman; a sweetly pretty and sexily beguiling child smile, all big eyes and long dark hair. Norman said: "You'll be all right." She said: "Isn't it a lovely day again?" Then she cast a smile at Caroline to avoid giving offence, but Caroline was giving her attention to something else. The white catamaran was coming up fast. Norman saw what she was looking at.

"Bloody fool. That'll never get through. You can't sail forty-foot cats on the Wey. That job's as broad as it is long."

A man further down waved the cat away: "You can't come through here!" Others were calling, helpfully, knowledgeably, matily, warningly: "You can't come through here!" Of everybody at the Thames lock waiting moorings, families, lovers, sailors, canoeists, from rubber dinghies to fibre-glass speedboats and every shape of small cabin cruiser, only Caroline Latimer knew that the catamaran did not want to go fucking through. They just wanted to shoot Caroline Latimer before she vanished out of their reach.

She said: "I'm going in to get out of the sun. It might help my head."

Norman said: "Why don't you make up the bed, darling? Strip right off and have a nice sleep. I'm sure I can manage."

"Later, perhaps," she said. She took the sailing book into the cabin with her and the pretty flags. There was a gun with telescopic sights already aligned with her bra strap, one could feel it. Her plan was to make contact with her killers. She had to make friends with Sycamore before the lock gates began to open; they would never allow her to take the horn into Surrey or anywhere else. The women and perhaps the men being used as cock-bait were obviously very carefully chosen. Mrs Glen's was just the place to find people with that much social conscience. They were not accustomed to recruits walking out. She turned the pages of the nautical book finding nothing she wanted. Then she glanced into the index under F for flags and soon there it was—a life-saver. When she came out into the cockpit Norman Drake and Jenny from the next boat were dangling their legs together on the bank.

"Oh," said Norman. The couple moved a little apart. "You feeling better, Caroline?"

She was waiting to be shot; she could see the muzzle of the gun gleaming inside the open porthole of the catamaran—unless she was looking at the porthole on the other side, a ring withing a ring, as it were.

"I thought I would just like to fly a flag. Do you mind?"

"No, of course not. Good idea. Mind you don't put up something that says Smallpox Aboard!"

They all laughed and Caroline put up something that said: "I may need your assistance."

The muzzle of the gun vanished; or somebody shut a porthole.

The very thin, very pretty girl who looked as though she was modelling cabin cruisers, was saying: "It must be exciting. Following them everywhere. And dangerous, these days. Who are you following now?"

Norman was embarrassed that Caroline had heard this, had caught him royalty dropping. "Ah, I'm not allowed to say." He said it waggishly but also seriously, and then luckily Jenny's boy friend Petey came back and the gates began to open, the flood moving the river like heavy treacle. Petey pulled his girl from the bank and from her new friend as if he was accustomed to doing it. "We shall be all right. They're giving us more water."

Jenny said: "Oh good. This is Norman. This is Petey. I don't know your friend's name. You're wife's name. Well—"

"Caroline," Norman explained. "I think we're off. Okay, Caroline? Let me start the motor before you untie."

"There's been an accident up at Cox's Lock," Petey was saying as they got back aboard their craft. The catamaran which had not actually moored anywhere was now moving in a circle with four blasts on its horn followed by a pause then one blast for a starboard turnabout.

"I should think so too," said Norman. "Bloody battleship." He had apparently not connected the cat with the one they had moored against at Platt's Eyot. Or else he had and found nothing significant in it. Somebody aboard the cat waved towards them. Caroline knew then that she had been accepted back on Elsie's copulating angels-of-mercy roster. Any assistance she needed would now be carried out by road. This was her interpretation. As they moved in line behind Petey's motor-sailer they heard the couple quarreling. Voices in the sun, in the water.

"Well, you're wrong, Petey. His girl was there the whole time. Anyway, I haven't got a telephone number—only yours now."

"It's a little boy."

"What, drowned?"

"Dunno. There's three police launches gone up. . ."

Their own voices as they waited for the basin to fill again. "More wine, Caroline?" "Not yet. I got really squiffy for a time." "Yes, I did. It's good stuff. A swim, that's what we need. It's clean up here. The water, I mean." "Is it, Norman?"

Did it, Norman, Are you, Norman, Was it, Norman, Can I, Norman, Really, Norman, Shall we, Norman, And recurring and recurring and recurring, is what you had to hold yourself in and be like and do and say and think if you wanted a weekly screw in return for a nightly screw and a house and garden and car and forget your fucking BA and Thomas-fucking-More and Jimmy-the-fucking-Weazel and all those poor fucking caught-by-the-balls bankrupts and getting fucking hit, hit, hit all the fucking time.

"Did you hear her? That girl on the boat in front. She thought we were married."

"Prophetic," said Caroline Latimer.

"Eh? What? Sorry?"

"Pathetic, I said. Young people thinking like that. Brainwashed. I bet she gives him a baby if he doesn't come up to scratch, Old Petey. He looks a bit of a bloody rebel. Those little homely bearded ones with a convict's cap and a fierce eye. She might find herself riding a tiger."

"She looks as though she could take care of it."

Dialogues in a flooding lock basin on a hot summer's day. The Goodyear airship has gone down like the sun.

"Let go the lines, sweetie."

"Aye aye, Petey."

Caroline laughed: "I think they're rather sweet."

"So do I," said Norman Drake. "I'm glad you do. You see, I never had a family of my own." He meant, only the royals. "I was an orphan."

You poor fucking slob, Caroline Latimer thought. "And haven't you ever been married, Norman?" They got their lines and moved out of the basin before he answered that one. When it came, she felt certain, he would say something guaranteed to get her knickers off. He said: "I was rather badly let down."

"Were you, Norman?"

In the little River Wey it seemed that the boat had got bigger; both shores seemed to be within jumping distance. Sailing now needed more concentration and Norman Drake applied himself to it, keeping to what he judged to be the deepest part of the channel, reducing his clearances with the downstream craft to avoid hitting the starboard shoals. She lay, a hand up under his T-shirt and on his bare back.

"Don't think about it. . ."

Norman gave Caroline a grateful smile. This was her first positive move towards being a fucking virgin. Somewhere deep in her legal thinking, down among the torts, she had the niggling knowledge that a boy had fallen in somewhere up ahead. She was refusing to connect it with Timothy or the red lettuce; she was refusing to take the blame until she knew more. Ashore all kinds of emergency noises were going—bells, sirens—like any old movie in the next room.

The river is not a part of this noisome world.

10

Sycamore sat in a sleek limousine ambulance with dark glass windows. It was parked off the carriageway by the side of Black Boy bridge, half a mile below Cox's Lock. Behind the wheel was a policeman in chauffeur's uniform named Gordon Crouch, who had the horn. He had a thin, boy's face, tired with too much therapy. Beside him sat Captain Andrew Turner with his port-wine eye, looking grim. He had one arm over into the back, his hand on the policewoman Elsie's vagina, holding her in readiness for another casualty, working her up into some kind of lubricatory state.

"I think that will be all right, Andy," she said.

"You don't want to be dry. Remember Lucan the first time?" They had pseudonyms for victims, rather than risk libel actions. Lucan was the worst horn in the whole epidemic. He had raped her while she was doing a crossword puzzle, all unprepared. Old, rich people, had taken to the rabbits' revenge as the aristocracy took to opium when rumour had it that Queen Victoria was considering adding China to India and drawing-rooms were flooding with chinoiserie.

"Here they come, sir. No it's not."

"I wish you wouldn't keep saying that, Crouch."

"Sorry, sir. I'm getting a bit horny again, sir. With you doing that. Couldn't she put her knickers on, sir?"

"With any luck you can have Miss Latimer soon. I think she got the message loud and clear. Pity she had to shoot Trotter. He was a good man."

Turner looked at his watch. "Two miles at four knots—give them twenty minutes at the Weybridge lock. If they haven't stopped they ought to be here."

"There's nowhere to stop, is there?" Elsie said. "Not for a how-d'you-do. Isn't it bloody funny—everybody tries to use the lettuce for personal reasons soon as they know about it. I did. Dobbin did. Poor old Dobbin. I wonder what his mum's going to do?"

"Action stations!" snapped Captain Andrew Turner.

Norman Drake's *Dolphin* had rounded the bend in the strong hot early evening sunlight and was heading down towards the bridge, its flags flying. The chauffeur said: "I think I've got a blue on." Elsie said: "Well, come over here for a little minute." "Stay where you bloody are. And you, Elsie, shut up and keep your juices going." She lay back and started work; she hated masturbating.

Turner now had his binoculars on the passing boat. "That's funny. I don't think she's given it to him yet. He's not holding his balls."

"Who is he?" asked Crouch.

"Don't know. They're checking. He picked her up, so it's nobody she set out to lay. She may not have blown the works. We'll get him in for interrogation."

"I'm not doing all this for nothing, am I?" asked Elsie.

"Give it another half hour and you can have Crouch."

"Oh, Christ!" said the chauffeur, holding on tight.

"I know, I know," said the captain. "You've got to learn to live with it." "And finish up like poor old Ben Dobbin," said Crouch. Elsie said, comfortingly: "They'll get something for it. They must. There's got to be. Else we'll all be wiped out like the rabbits."

"They're shooting them in Russia," said Crouch.

"We're not Russia and never were," said Captain Turner. "They haven't got national health."

Crouch said: "Look at 'em. She's bloody sunbathing."

Caroline Latimer had passed beneath them and gone on upstream, spreadeagled on the cabin roof and covered in a rosy warm light.

"Don't be fooled," said the captain. He was keeping her in focus as long as possible. "That's an unusual girl. She's got a chip on her shoulder, that girl. Shoots like Buffalo Bill. And she's got enough red lettuce up her bikini to make this river stand up on end."

"What we gonna do, captain?" asked Crouch.

Captain Andrew Turner spoke without removing his eyes from his target. "I want that girl in my team."

Sycamore, at this point in time, Caroline Latimer would explain in her well-known lecture, knew nothing of Timothy or Lady Catherine Vesey or Warren Morgan the solicitor. They were aware that there had been a police alert, but it did not appear to be connected with their own private and secret mission.

11

Still far from Guildford and her fucking whore of a mother and impotent vegetarian father, at 6.30 on this same super Sunday evening, Caroline Latimer and Norman Drake were swimming in the Wey Navigation a quarter mile upstream from Cox's Lock. The water was a bit dirty from being churned over mud by so many boats, but it was not unhealthy. Before letting herself down off the boat, now staked to the bank, Caroline watched the sturdy young policeman with his potato face swim strongly back and forth across the river three complete times without stopping.

"Well?" she asked, when he came back and hung on at her feet.

"Beautiful. Come in. Quite clean. Fishing down there. Phew." He spat into the water.

"All right, then," she said. She slid her bottom over the side and he helped her in, laughing as she gasped at the coldness. The hotter the body the colder the water. If she had a period she wouldn't be doing this, he thought. She thought: he's wearing his Y-fronts. That means he's got nothing to put on afterwards either. They splashed each other and laughed and exchanged smiles with passing people and soon they were ready to come out. Rather than face the mud and weeds of the bank they went up on the boat, Norman first in order to help her. They sat washing their feet clean, the water still running down them, the sun still warm enough to make them steam.

Caroline said: "One gets so invigorated swimming."

"I don't know about you, but I'm starving."

She said: "I could do with something. I expect mummy's

keeping dinner." He said: "Come inside and dry off, Caroline." She said: "What about you?" He said: "Well, I'm afraid there's only one towel—the one you've been lying on. I'll follow you with it." The small protocol of drying themselves became more important than the cure for cancer. They both swung their legs over into the cockpit and he reached up and pulled the orange-and-black smelly towel from the sun-deck. He draped it protectively around her shoulders and kept his arms around her, patting her dry as he gently pushed her towards the cabin. She resisted this, holding him back and taking the towel to herself.

"I can manage, Norman."

He said: "Are you sure?" But he remained in the cockpit and she went down the companionway and into the cabin. He said: "I'll put the canopy up a minute. Bit of privacy."

"Good idea," she called.

Norman Drake pulled the heavy canvas hood to cover the cockpit, then zipped up the side-curtains, shutting out the Wey Navigation and leaving them cosy in a two-room shaded world. He took off his wet pants and mopped himself all over with his T-shirt. The cold water had shrunk his balls and penis to nothing. The foreskin had come up to cover the tip and the hairs surrounded it all and it had the look of something fossilised that would be quite useless until reconstituted. Suddenly her hand came out of the doorway holding her wet bra and panties and his cock jerked in its prison.

"Put these somewhere to dry, Norman."

"Okay, darling." And when he had, he said: "Can I come in?"

"Just a sec."

"I'm counting, honey," he said. He got as far as five and went into the cabin. Caroline had been expecting this and had put on her chiffon dress as far as her breasts; now she dropped it in the expert way she had, so that he saw her naked for a moment, and then barely covered in filmy nothing which clung to her damp body, her pants and bra outside and her slip in Sunbury General Hospital laundry. Norman made a passionate lunge for her. She side-stepped and thrust the big damp towel at him with a mischievous: "Toro!" His penis was sticking out like an inquisitive long-necked bird from its nest and appeared to be looking at her. She said, authoritatively: "Dry off and put your trousers on while I get the food."

"Bugger food," said the detective.

She had to avoid him again and said: "Then if you are very good you can dry my hair for me. It takes a lot of rubbing."

"Do you mean it?"

"Of course. Outside in the sunshine."

"In here!"

They stared at each other for a little; she had to give in or be raped. "All right—in here. But first I'm starving."

She became busy with the food, clearing a space, opening the refrigerator, taking out crockery. Reluctantly Detective Inspector Norman Drake put his white flannel trousers on, running his finger up and down the fly zip to avoid catching hairs.

"Here," she said. She handed him a glass of red wine and filled her own, touched glasses with him.

Their eyes met again and Caroline Latimer, her contact lenses safely in her bag, felt that she had never been so desired, not even by Dobbin. Certainly not by Warren Morgan the solicitor who had used her abominably. He watched her chopping up tomato and lettuce and pâté and bread and he sipped his wine and he earmarked the bunk where he was soon going to lay her on her back.

"Do you like celery?" she asked.

He said: "I love celery. You know what they say about celery!"

"You cunt," she thought.

"I want to make love to you, Caroline," said Norman Drake.

"Do you, Norman?"

"Come and sit here."

They sat together on the bunk, their food on their laps, glasses on the floor. Each time she stooped to get her glass he could see one nipple. He said: "There hasn't been anybody since Deborah." They were talking through their chewing, bum to bum, knee to knee, everything getting closer.

"Tell me 'bout it. Have some chutney on that cheese."

Norman had some chutney and said: "She was a police sergeant. Beautiful girl from Temple Fortune. Jewish, you know."

Caroline said, "You're not Jewish, are you? Oh no," she added, obscurely, but in fact remembering his foreskin.

"We were all ready to get married. I mean presents were coming in. Three electric blankets. You know. Well, we'd been courting five years. There was a police house waiting for us until we got a mortgage."

"What happened?"

"She changed."

"Was there somebody else?"

"No. That's what everybody said. Nobody else. She told me. She still loved me. She was broken-hearted."

"Have some more cheese. I don't understand, Norman."

"No, I don't either, Caroline."

"Can I ask you something?" said Caroline Latimer. And when she could she said: "Did Deborah have a dog?"

"A dog? Her family had a dog. She wasn't an animal girl."

Caroline munched, gloomily: "I got jilted for a fucking alsatian."

Norman put his arm right round her and held her port-side nipple: "Please don't swear, Caroline."

She pushed away from him by putting her hand down seemingly accidentally right on his hard penis and seemingly not realising it and keeping it there; he kept hold of her nipple. "Sorry, Norman," she said. "It's a habit. You'll have to try to get me out of it. Fine me ten-p every time I swear. Tell me about Deborah." She let go of his cock and picked up a piece of white celery.

In return he released her nipple. He said: "Have you ever heard of Sycamore?"

Caroline stopped everything to look at him.

He took this for blank ignorance and said: "It's a para-military organisation. British. Connected with the police. Deborah joined them."

"Oh, I see." She did indeed see.

"They were desperate for women and offering something like double normal police pay. Well, danger money. It's anti-terrorist, I believe. She was out all hours and coming home a wreck. I mean, we were living together for a time but it became useless. She was worn out. You won't believe this but sometimes she used to sleep for thirty-six hours at a stretch! We didn't have sex for three months and when we did she had these terrible pains. She wouldn't go to a doctor. Then all at once she got transferred down to Cornwall. I haven't seen her since. One card from St Ives—that was Christmas last year."

"I am sorry, Norman."

Norman ran a hand up her thigh: "Now I've got you."

"Eat up," she said.

"Her father thinks she went down there to have a baby. Someone she works with. She won't let anybody go down there and see her. Never gives her postal address—only a box number."

"One has the right to live one's own life," said Caroline.

"What I've been wanting, Caroline—what I've been needing for a long time is a really sincere, strong relationship."

Norman Drake had finished eating and he had finished drinking and he was ready to get it in. She said: "I'll just clear these things away and you can give me a rub. If you want to, Norman."

Norman shook the towel and judged the precise place for him to sit on the bunk seat. The boat rocked in the wash of a passing craft and clearly they heard the pips for the seven o'clock news. "In Surrey this afternoon the hunt is on for a missing child..." The sound of the engine drowned the BBC voice. Caroline came and sat where directed and tossed back her damp hair for him to work on. Norman Drake began rubbing her hair briskly with the towel, at the same time rubbing his crutch into her bottom. Once it had begun and the pattern of movement established, she allowed it to continue. She gave him two minutes to lose control— he did it in one-and-a-half. The first signal came when he lifted her hair from her shoulders and kissed first her ear and then her neck and quite soon manoeuvred to pull her back across his lap and kiss her mouth, his hands searching all her private places with the thoroughness of a policeman. She did not resist until his hand at last ran into her crutch and stopped to mould it, his fingers moving gently through the chiffon.

"Let me take this off for you, Caroline."

"Yes, Norman."

In sheer gratitude he kissed her more passionately before undressing her. He said: "I love you, you know, Caroline."

She said: "Do you, Norman?" Without her contact lenses and with his mouth on hers and his fingers in her vagina it all seemed thrillingly romantic and she was becoming increasingly reluctant to play her trump card. But it had to be done and before she was on her back with her legs open. One had to remember one's lifetime of futureless fucks and exercise a modicum of control. He was ripe for marriage and had probably still got the presents and the mortgage. One could suck a person off for the duration of a short engagement.

"Norman!" God almighty he had thrust into her from behind, chiffon and all. "Sorry, darling. Let's get this out of the way." She said: "And put the towel down." He said: "What?" "I'll do it," she said. He watched her spread the damp towel with its bright black and orange stripes where her bottom was to rest. He said: "But that's wet, Caroline." She said: "It can't be helped." Worried, he said: "Have you started your period?" She shook her head and somehow managed to look shy and evasive and a little frightened. Norman Drake could not believe what he was hearing until she suddenly yielded herself and drew him down on top of her, unzipping his fly at the same time. "Be gentle, Norman …"

Caroline had judged his character and his responses and his fears and priorities and prejudices to a pretty accurate degree. She felt his passion rising as he realised that he was about to penetrate a virgin in her middle twenties; and she felt his brain decline to go ahead. His equipment was hard and wet and well down into the open perimeters, but he held back.

"Are you telling me that this is the first time, darling?"

She sobbed and would not answer.

"Don't be ashamed," he whispered. "Don't be ashamed,

darling. I only love you the more. What stopped you living a normal life with your boy friend?"

"He didn't love me. He loved his fucking dog."

"Please don't swear, Caroline. You're so sweet and innocent. Do you want me inside you?"

"Yes. Yes, please! Please! Norman! Please!"

With this amount of passion and urgency his police mind would suspect that she was already probably pregnant and looking for a father. He said: "Let's do it another way. This time." She said the age-old things: "It's not fair on you, Norman." And as they progressed, coming and half-coming with mutual masturbatory techniques of tongue and hand and even arse hole, she said: "I know I'm silly, a virgin at twenty-four," dropping a couple of years somewhere, or: "Perhaps when we know each other better." Nobody ever says "You can fuck me if you marry me first," because this would be, one supposes, prostitution, as recommended in the bible. Even so, when one is a squint-eyed spinster graduate coming up to 28 or more, that is what one fucking requires. She could see Norman Drake going bald and doing the front lawn as his face was down at her vagina again, his tongue busy on the clit. He would have a beer belly and brewer's droop by forty; she could pick and choose her love life. So much easier with a decent bedroom to ask them into and no motive or money hassles—a bit of official receiving on the side. She would get her judge. Effingham was good for judges. She reached another orgasm—my God, what a super weekend—pulling his hair in ecstasy.

"It's no use," he said suddenly. "Sorry, darling."

He came up on her, ran his hard cock straight into her steaming wet vagina, punching away as if to make up for the whole afternoon.

"Norman! Norman, no! You're not wearing anything! Get off me you bastard! You'll give me a baby! Where's your french letter?"

"It's across there," he said, now that he had come up towards orgasm and was riding to make it last. "Too late now. If you're pregnant I'll marry you."

"You won't! You fucking won't!"

"Let's talk about it afterwards, darling. God you're lovely. You're wonderful. You're marvellous. I love you. I love you. I love you." All more or less coxwain's in-out, in-out, in-out phraseology to keep time with the oldest dance in the world.

She said: "If you come inside me I shall scream. Norman, did you hear me? Norman!"

And then she screamed and screamed and Sycamore rushed in, having been already aboard and waiting for it. Captain Andrew Turner and Crouch and Elsie. Turner pulled at Norman Drake but could not shift him until the orgasm was completed and safely inside Caroline. It was the beginning of her lecture-tour pregnancy. Then Norman Drake was held and chloroformed and transported out to the ambulance. It had been pushed by hand across the grass from the towpath. With everyone out of the way the leather-coated Sycamore man gave Caroline Latimer time to put on her dress, lighting a cigarette meanwhile and holding desultory chat.

"You did well, Miss Latimer. Clever thing, those signals. Lot of initiative." He scanned the remains of the salad. "How much lettuce did he eat— we like to keep medical statistics." She said: "Do you mind stepping outside while I wipe my cunt?" He said: "Sorry. So sorry. Don't be long. We have to get him somewhere safe before he comes round."

She ignored the implications of this and said: "Would you mind seeing if my underclothes are dry—they're hanging somewhere in the rigging."

The captain went in search and handed them in to her, then remained discreetly out of sight while she did her things, but within talking distance. "Well, you've given us a good old run, Caroline. If I may call you Caroline. Andy's my name, since you're joining us. Andy Pandy, never randy. Doesn't do to be with all this going on around you."

"Have you got the horn?" Caroline asked, politely. She felt better in knickers and bra, more in control.

"No, thank heavens," he said. "One needs to be objective to be effective. That's why I could do with a good effective woman like yourself. You've caused havoc already. I like that."

She was nearly ready to be seen. "What sort of havoc?" Her

hair was a lost cause; all that in-fighting while it was still damp. She brushed at it and listened to the captain's voice.

"Dobbin and Trotter both dead and heaven knows what's going to happen to this chap. Not a bad start, eh?"

Caroline Latimer stopped brushing her hair and went out into the covered cockpit; the captain appraised her, warmly.

"Smashing. That's a very pretty dress. But you ought to wear spectacles instead of those contacts. Glasses would suit you—shorten you nose."

She said, "Thank you, captain." She sat down by the tiller then and looked up at him, apprehensively. "Dead? Dobbin?"

"'Fraid so. He got back off duty and found you'd taken his lettuce and not left your telephone number. In his condition that was enough. Sometimes getting a puncture is enough to cause suicide. Poor old Ben couldn't take it. Mutilated himself in a bath of warm water. Not pretty. Not pretty at all. And not the first, either. There've been a score country-wide. They start seeing their organ as another person they can't get rid of. Some of them are completely disoriented. Crouch is going that way. My driver. Then we have to send them down to Ding Dong. Have a cigarette? That's the end of the road, I'm afraid. That's in Cornwall. Where they grow the beastly stuff."

He lit her a tipped Camel and at the same time: "Trotter you shot through the head. Fantastic on a quick draw. Well, he was trying to kill you. On my orders. Tit for tat." He laughed and expected her to laugh too, but she didn't. "You'd better sign up with us now even if it's only part-time. It's not just fucking, you know, there's lots of other interesting things. Do you like sucking off?"

"Sometimes," said Caroline. "But I find it hard to dissociate orgasm from love-making as you seem to do. You make it sound like a good shit."

He snapped his fingers at her in instant appreciation: "That's it. You've done it in one. And you and others like you are the enema. It's constipation, it's cancer, it's gangrene and finally it's a stump." He placed a hand on her shoulder and said, earnestly: "You're needed, Caroline. Make no mistake. We've got plenty of good women who never get their legs

together, but no leader. You could be our Florence Nightingale."

"Captain! Andy! Come quick! It's gone down!" Elsie had appeared at the cortain of the cockpit cover, pulling it back. "Come and see! Quick, in case it goes up again. Gordon's looking for a camera."

"Come on, you'd better see this," Andy Turner said to Caroline, helping her ashore by the hand. They ran to the ambulance and climbed into the. back. Norman Drake, still unconscious, was lying on the stretcher bed still in his white trousers, still with the fly unzipped and no pants underneath. His cock had flopped dismally down to the left-hand side and PC Crouch, tense with excitement, kept pulling it into a better position for photographing.

"Look at it, sir! It's gone down. This is what we've been waiting for all this time." He was crying and at the same time trying to align his camera and flash.

Elsie said to Caroline: "We've hoped for this, you see. It's what happened to the rabbits and myxomatosis—they got immunised. Oh, God, if only this is the beginning. What do you think, sir?"

"It's got to be! It's got to be! It's got to be!" sobbed Crouch, with each exclamation taking another picture of Norman's penis.

"Take a grip on yourself, man!" said the captain, sternly. "Let us think this thing out. It's no good jumping to conclusions. How can a man be immunised if he's only just had his first red lettuce?"

Elsie said: "You don't know it's his first, Andy." And to Caroline: "Did he say? I mean, had he got the horn when you met, did you notice?" Caroline said: "I don't honestly know— he's a policeman." This news sent Crouch into hysterics:

"There you are, then! The force is riddled with it. They've been using us as guinea pigs. Well, it's starting to wear off. Look at it!" He flicked Norman's dormant organ up and down with his finger. "Oh Christ, let me have one like that! I'll never want another fuck, God, I promise!"

Captain Turner punched his chauffeur in the face, knocking

116

him the length of the ambulance. When Crouch looked up from the floor he found that Captain Turner had a gun in his hand. Caroline could not quite believe what was happening.

"No, Andy," said Elsie. "Give him a chance. And anyway, I can't drive."

The captain said: "I'm sorry about this, Crouch. You've been a good man but now you've broken. You're no good to Sycamore and we can't have you spreading the gospel."

Crouch had his hand on his balls. "My cock's going down! It is. Come and feel, sir!"

He got no farther than that when the gun exploded, softly, silenced, leaving a vivid hole in the constable's head above his eyes.

Andy turned to Caroline: "I'm really sorry you had to see that, Caroline. So early. Look at his cock, Elsie, take the exact time and make a note. Statistics," he explained to Caroline.

She watched Elsie open the dead man's flies and saw the stiff hard penis come out, still blue at the end, still insatiable.

"His imagination was playing him tricks," Andy explained.

Elsie said: "I get really fed up with this job, sometimes. Gordon was really chuffed. You make a discovery and you get shot for it."

"There was no discovery, Elsie. Stiff-cock immunity is pie in the sky. You know it, I know it. I tell you why this man's cock has gone down. No, you tell her, Caroline."

He met Caroline's eyes for a moment and she knew that he knew already. She said: "He hasn't had any red lettuce."

"Oh, gawd!" said Elsie. "What a freeze. Poor old Gordon."

"He had his moment of hope," said the captain. Then he looked at Caroline. "All right, Caroline. What did you do with Dobbin's lettuce?" He was still, without threat one would assume, holding his silenced revolver.

A woman screamed outside: "Augustus come away from that water!"

"Most of it's in my refrigerator at home."

"Yes, we've got that. But you did make a red lettuce salad for somebody? Who was it? Somebody you're in love with who doesn't fancy you?"

Elsie said: "You'd better say, dear. If you're in love with him. You'll cripple him for life if you give him that lettuce. He won't just want you. He'll want fucking every six hours regularly except when he's under sedation. Soon he won't have orgasms and then you won't have babies. That's what it's all about. In Russia the population's dropping, the birth rate plummeting. They've set up freak farms for experimenting and extermination camps for the lost causes. In Russia the peasants' pricks are covered in hair. You go down to Ding Dong, you'll see what I mean."

Captain Turner said: "We're dropping them down the old tin mines. That reminds me, Elsie—get Crouch booked for the next consignment." And to Caroline: "If there's any more casualties you haven't mentioned you'd better tell me. There's a cattle train leaving for Penzance tomorrow morning. Two refrigerator trucks for the corpses."

"The mind positively boggles," said Caroline Latimer. In a few hours time she would be in the Royal Courts of Justice interrogating her bankrupts or taking tea with Jimmy the Weazel, all lucky men with little limp cocks if only they knew it. She began to feel as Alice must have felt on the bad days; if only she could find another kind of mushroom and wake up.

"I'm waiting, Miss Latimer," said Captain Andrew Turner.

"Timothy," said Caroline at last, and very reluctantly indeed. "Timothy something. I don't recall his surname. His mother lives at Godalming."

The officer looked very cynical. His eyebrow didn't rise or anything, but something happened to his birthmark. It turned deeper purple because of the wrinkles around his eye muscle. He did not have to do more than this for people to get the point.

Caroline Latimer got the point. "I know it sounds unbelievable, Captain Turner. Andy."

He said: "You can only call me Andy if you're going to say sensible things to me. Now then. Elsie give that chap another slosh of chloroform. Try not to kill him. Now then, Caroline. Make sense. You didn't steal that lettuce from poor Dobbin— you were his last fuck, incidentally—and take it home to

Highgate and concoct a picnic and then lead us a dance right across London to Hampton just to try and screw somebody whose name you don't even know and whose mother lives at Godalming. And then go up the river with somebody else. By the way I've got a dossier coming in on him. He's a crook, you know."

"He's a police officer."

"He's a crook. A villain. He steals boats. Him and Nigel Fry. Norman picks the craft, Nigel finds the customer. Hans Andersen got that from the river police when you first took off this afternoon. He doesn't like you, does he, the South African? I sent him back to Hampstead."

"Fecking good riddance," said Caroline. Did Dobbin know him? Of course Dobbin knew him. He'd called him Hans Andersen. All that guitar-playing and singing. One felt just a modicum of resentment that one had not been actually chosen. Especially at Mrs Glen's where there was not that much competition. And if Raymond de Freitas was in Sycamore, how about Mrs Glen? How about every fucking body? Now Norman Drake had feet of clay. She wished to God she'd put her cap in now. She was half-sitting at the end of his stretcher bed and he lay beside her like a cold potato. She remembered something important but suddenly decided it was best not to talk.

"You were going to say something?" Captain Turner said.

Caroline sighed; one's thoughts were not one's own any more. She said: "This man was waving to the police." She had to be careful here if she was not to divulge too much. "Giving them some sort of signal with his hankie. When a boat passed. The police followed it. That's when I first saw him."

Andy and Elsie looked at each other; the way two straight coppers feel about a bent copper. "Really? I see," said Andrew Turner. "Did you happen to notice the number on the police launch?"

Caroline said: "Of course not."

"And what about the other boat?" Elsie asked.

Taken off-guard Caroline said: "It was called the Merrymaker." She stopped talking, in such a way that it was obvious that she knew more. She had to go on to try to allay suspicion. "A little cream cabin cruiser. I think it was a Micro-Plus."

The captain stared at her in silence for long enough to make her nervous and rub her itchy eyes. "How would you know all that?"

Fuck, shit, damn, cunt, areshole and cunnilingus, thought the Official Receiver's examiner in bankruptcy. Nevertheless she told them everything. She mentioned Martin and the bishops and the queenery and Keats Restaurant and laid it all at the door of Warren Morgan the solicitor.

She was halfway through the flea-bitten fucking alsatian dog when she was stopped effectively by Andy's hand over her mouth. She squinted up at him with her evil squint. He removed his hand a split second before she had time to bite it.

"Sorry about that, Caroline, but it's old ground. We know all about your troubles. You wouldn't have been picked if you hadn't been investigated first thoroughly."

"Still, he is a bleeder from all accounts," Elsie said. "I read the dossier on you. You should have been tougher right from the start. You could have slipped that bloody dog some arsenic, surely?"

The captain said: "That's not very nice."

"Bloody men," Elsie said. "Treat 'em mean, keep 'em keen. Don't worry, dear. I don't blame you for wanting to try the red lettuce on him."

"You see, Timothy was just a try-out. I wasn't sure how much it took or how long. Then he arrived with Catherine and orf they went."

The two members of Sycamore looked confused. "When was this, Caroline?" asked the captain. "We've had you under surveillance all day."

"This afternoon when the pubs closed."

Elsie said: "I was watching you then. You were cleaning up this boat and making it nice."

"Not this boat, Elsie. Timothy's boat. The Merrymaker."

"Here!" the girl said suddenly, a confused memory stirring. "Did you get off one boat and get on another?"

"Yes."

Elsie was depressed and so was her boss. She said: "I missed that. I must have dropped off. Well, I've been at it all day. Where are they now?"

"Somewhere up ahead. They're going to Godalming. Yes, and that's another thing. Lady Catherine's aboard—the Duke of Waterlow's daughter. Norman's her personal security officer. Or one of them. He helped save the princess from the kidnappers. Catherine Vesey is a Lady-in-Waiting."

Captain Turner considered this for a moment. "She won't have to wait long if Timothy's eaten that fucking lettuce. Excuse my language. I think we've been following the wrong boat. You could get dismissed the service for this, Elsie."

"That would be a bloody rest."

"You haven't answered my question," Caroline said. "How would Norman Drake know who she was were he not a *bona fide* officer? I think you're making a mistake about him."

"Listen, I'm not making any mistake. He's a crook. It's his job to know who people are. If he was interested in their Micro-Plus it's because Nigel Fry has got a customer for it. I'm not saying there's not a few coppers involved."

"And another thing," said Caroline.

"We don't want any more things, Miss Latimer. Elsie, get on the blower and fetch Nick and his dog down here. When this chap wakes up, interrogate him and let him go."

"What am I going to tell him? You can't just chloroform members of the public for making love on their own boat."

Captain Andrew Turner was not listening to the women now. Something he had recently said remained in his mind but was too frightful for swift mental resolution. The women went on talking together for a moment or two.

Caroline was saying to Elsie: "Norman's girl friend worked for Sycamore. He didn't know what it was, but I did. I recognised the job."

Elsie said: "What was her name, dear?"

"I don't know. Yes, I do. Deborah—"

"Deborah! That's Deborah Calvert. She was with the river police before she volunteered. She's down at Ding Dong now.

Don't get brothelised, Caroline. It's more stubs than pricks down there now. You never get off your back—what are you doing, Andy. Don't kick him!"

Wrapped in fearful speculation the captain sat kicking the dead Crouch in the head with an absently swinging toe-cap. "Stop yacking you two and listen," he said. "I think we're in trouble."

Caroline Latimer was not unaware of what that trouble was, but she had no intention of betraying her guilty secret.

Andy said to her now: "Did you say your Timothy was a bit half-and-half?"

"I think so."

"And do you know what the red lettuce can do to queers?"

"One would suppose they go for other queers."

"Has it occurred to you that your Timothy might be a pederast?"

"Please don't keep calling him 'my' Timothy."

"You see what I'm getting at, don't you?" And in case they didn't, he made it plain. "An innocent child is missing somewhere not far from here."

"Oh dear!" said Caroline.

"Oh dear?" said Andy. "Oh dear? Unless I miss my bet that boy's fate is the first classic case of the krasniy latouk effect in homosexuals."

This was the first time Caroline encountered the words krasniy latouk. She became aware of the red lettuce case-histories supplied by Leningrad university's department of bio-chemistry. In her later work for the public relations team who took over from Sycamore screwing and lecturing, at Ding Dong and elsewhere, she was able to absorb what literature was at that time available and even contribute to it on the basis of her own experiences. Her Women's Lib book, *The Redundant Cock*, became something of a bible. It was translated into seven languages, accidentally won the science fiction prize, led to new legislation making the dealing in red lettuce off prescription a prisonable offence with a maximum sentence of ten years. The book also led to the setting up of the Caroline Latimer Semen Bank Against Fuck Famine (CLSBAFF). The search for Timothy

Tite—as his name turned out to be—was a significant turning point in the adventures of Caroline, that super weekend on the river. For the first time she became cognisant of the full terrifying prognosis of that terrible rabbit weed.

"You come with me, Caroline," Captain Andy said, at last, with almost piratical fervour, glad to be moving into action. "Elsie, you stay here and take care of things this end. Put poor Crouch out of sight before Mr Drake comes round. Let Nick know what's happened. We may very well need reinforcements before the night's out. We've got to find this maniac before the locals find him or it'll be Lucan over again. Murder, rape and torture are one thing, but you can't go dropping children's bodies down tin mines in this country. Which makes England what she is, thank God."

Caroline had listened to all this with growing misgivings. She said, tentatively: "Would you mind awfully if I didn't come? I really would like to just get a Green Line to Guildford. Mummy was having some friends in to dinner. I need a bath and some clean clothes—" What she really needed was a good shit again but his hand was already over her mouth—just long enough to quash any hopes of escape she might have.

Andy said: "I don't think you understand, Caroline. This is a national emergency. You'll have plenty of time for a mummy night afterwards."

Elsie, getting more and more upset, said: "Look here, Andy, is she taking my place as your Number Two?"

"No, no, no, no, no, no, no! Oh, fuck me. Women. Caroline knows the boat, she knows the couple—that's assuming the girl's still alive—I need her. We've got to put a dragnet on this river while the light still lasts." Then, more gently, holding Elsie's hand: "You are needed here, darling. Look at the time. When you've got rid of this chap—just send him back to his boat and tell him his girl's gone home—Nick is going to want servicing."

"Oh, fuck!" Elsie said. "I've been lubricating my cunt all the afternoon, now I've got Nick. He's as dry as a bone, not to mention that bloody dog Tiger."

"Tiger?" said Andy. "Don't you have that bloody dog on

your back. I've issued memos to everybody. That dog is spoilt. You tell Nick I said so. Dogs shouldn't be eating the lettuce. They're supposed to just sniff it. If we've got to fight animal erections let the RSPCA set up a special dog branch. Ready, Caroline?"

Caroline said: "We don't really have to search that far, Andy." The thought of being fucked by the incurably stiff prick of a fully-grown alsatian was positively mind-boggling. It was far beyond the call of any Florence Nightingale she could recall. Her desperate Official Receiver's mind came up with one of those tiny recollections that sometimes sent bankrupts to prison, hoist by their own petard. In the self-perpetuating factory of her brain Caroline Latimer kept the kind of tiny electronic detail that held jets in flight and ships on course.

"Do you know a pub called *The Jolly Farmer?*" she said. As he and Elsie thought about it over the bodies of the unconscious Norman Drake and the dead Gordon Crouch and his dead stiff cock, she added: "I promised Catherine Vesey I might be there about eight o'clock. She was just a tiny bit dubious about Timothy."

"Leave me some cigarettes," Elsie said as they left her.

"Up front in the cubby hole with the vaseline," Captain Andy Turner told her. Left alone, the young policewoman sat down by Norman's feet and held her crutch, crying softly, rocking herself to and fro.

12

"Petey …"

"Yes, sweetie?"

"Can we afford a Snowball?"

"No. You drink bitter. Boaty girls drink bitter."

"Oh, Petey …"

"Excuse me. You probably don't remember me? At Thames Lock? Waiting for the gates to open?"

Sweetie and Petey looked at Caroline Latimer, this tired-looking young woman in long, crumpled chiffon, her hair lank and damp and tangled, her eyes slightly cast, her voice over-carefully middle-class to hide her desperation. Sweetie remembered her, but Petey didn't.

"You were with that gorgeous man in an Alcatraz T-shirt." She explained to Peter in an aside: "Well, he was quite nice. Not as nice as you. Have you lost him?"

"May I sit down a minute?"

They were at those little tables that stand on the terrace and grass verges between *The Jolly Farmer* and the sandy-shored bend in the Wey Navigation between Guildford and Godalming. Caroline Latimer was only a ten-minute fast run from home and she had a gun in her handbag. Captain Turner was down by the water's edge looking for the Micro-Plus Merrymaker. He also had a gun, a knife, a hand-grenade and several kinds of dopes and deadly poisons in capsule form. Hit in the right place he would blow up.

"I'm just getting some drinks," said little bearded Petey. "Can I get you something?"

"I'd love a quick Snowball," said Caroline.

"Of course." There was a battle of glances with his crew, Jenny, or Sweetie, and he added: "Two large Snowballs."

"This is extremely kind of you," said Caroline. She worked it out that it was worth at least fifty pence; the first decent gain today.

"He can afford it," sweetie Jenny explained. "He's a famous photographer, really. We've just bought a new flat in Hampstead. Fitzjohns Avenue. We may get married. I want to have some babies but Petey wants a bigger boat. Are you in trouble?"

"I'm looking for somebody. A girl and a chap." Caroline was very close to tears, which is what had caused Jenny's sudden concern. It was the mention of Fitzjohns Avenue and Hampstead and that lovely normal life-size world up above the rabbit warren. Mrs Glen's and Elliot Frazer and Farquharson's coffee shop and Bubbles and Jek and Vorster and that little runtish girl in jeans and all the dull furniture of her postgraduate life, even the Thomas More bankruptcy building and Jimmy the Weazel and even Warren Morgan the solicitor and his rotten dog all seemed poignantly desirable and out of reach now. If ever she got back she resolved to be kinder to her fucking whore of a mother and the impotent C. H. Latimer.

"Tell me what they look like."

"The girl is Lady Catherine Vesey. She might be the queen one day."

"Good lord, how exciting. What does she look like?"

"She's a very pretty, sort of hockey-stick girl. She moves about very quickly and wears jeans and smokes fags, that sort of thing. She's wearing worn-out jeans and a funny little shrunken woollen jumper for some reason or other. Royalty don't have any dress sense, do they? But she's very nice. Always in the news. She's probably in one of these papers."

There were all the raggle taggle of abandoned Sunday papers around them and together they started browsing through and Petey came back with the drinks on a circular tin tray advertising Aspro.

"Caroline's looking for Lady Catherine Vesey," Jenny explained.

"What sort of boat has she got?" asked Petey.

Caroline said: "It's a Micro-Plus called The Merrymaker. Or just Merrymaker."

Petey said: "Cheers!" He drank, and then he said: "It's about two hundred yards downstream. Moored in a kind of cut. A mooring place overgrown with weeds and that. The girl off it is doing her nut. She's had three large brandies in the last half hour."

"*That* girl!" Jenny exclaimed. "Oh yes, of course it is. She's been searching everywhere, asking questions. Looking for you I expect."

"Where is she now?" Caroline asked.

"In the telephone kiosk near the front entrance of the pub."

"You'll catch her easily," said Jenny. "You know what telephones are. You can never get through."

"I'll just drink my drink," said Caroline Latimer.

Somehow she felt a little more in control again; less dragged around in handcuffs. She sat back and sipped her Snowball and crossed her legs and accepted a cigarette from Petey and watched Captain Andrew Turner making his way up-stream in the wrong direction, going from boat to boat and asking questions and sweating. At least Lady Kate was still alive; one less death on Caroline's conscience. She quite saw now the psychology of people like Hitler and General Amin and the Shah of Iran. Conscience was all a matter of degree. If one killed one or two less people on any particular day then one could feel quite saintly. Farmers had to kill rabbits and dictators had to kill people, but if it were all in some accepted common cause then a few weeks later people shook hands with one again. Looking back on it—and one could look back on things even while still in the bubbling middle of them—she most regretted the ghastly death of poor Dobbin. One fully intended to see people, but one simply forgot to leave one's telephone number. Particularly inside a marrow. She regretted killing Trotter but it was self-defence. He was doing his duty and she was stopping him. Later she took the trouble to go to Lewisham and put flowers on his grave. His name was Geoffrey Sainsbury, called Trotter after pigs' trotters, Sainsbury's being a famous chain butchers. She was reluctant at this moment, which is why she was wiping her finger around her glass to scoop the last of the advocaat, to discover too much about what her red lettuce had done to Timothy and what he might have done to some innocent child. If Lady Catherine had had three brandies and was frantic and was alone, then clearly the next few minutes would bring the unwelcome confirmation. One somehow expected private horrors to be limited to a private landscape.

"Where is your friend?" asked sweet Jenny. "Norman, wasn't it?"

"He's been chloroformed."

"Oh my word," said Jenny. Petey was waiting for the bald statement to turn into a joke, but it didn't. "By the police," Caroline told them. She got up and pulled her dress into some kind of reasonable shape. Without a slip it kept getting stuck up her arse. She picked up her large handbag with the gun in it and shook her little parasol and smiled at them, feeling very much better. "They thought he was a sex maniac."

"Gosh," said Jenny. "Let us know what happens. We're at Peterlee Studios in Beak Street. I'm Petey's model."

Caroline touched their hands. "Caroline Latimer. You can get me at the Royal Courts of Justice."

They watched her walk away through the river boozers and enter the conservatory door of *The Jolly Farmer*, a little crinoline lady caught in a dream.

"Look!" said Jenny. "That man's after her!" The burly Captain Turner in his black leathers and his red eye was hurrying to catch up with Caroline. Jenny said: "I bet she leads a jolly full life."

Petey looked at Sweetie with an expression that said that any man Sweetie flirted with was likely to be a sex maniac. He lowered the expression into his beer and she gave him an indulgent smile and held his hand for safety.

On that hot Sunday evening when Weenie's friend Norman Drake arrived and broke the news about her alarming adventures, C.H. was doing one of his funny turns on the back lawn by the fish pond. Christine next door got him at it. She was in her blue bikini, and quite apart from that I think m old man fancies her in his staid way. He had been pretending not to know that he was sprinkling her with his hose over the honeysuckle on the wattle fencing. It's very high and we all know that Chris does her sunbathing on the other side. Now she and her husband Reg, a dentist, had brough some vermouth and ice round and Reg was strumming a German march rhythm on his ukelele. C.H. rolls his trousers up for this one and goose-steps on the spot, something he did with the Footlights.

"Ach! Mein Gott!
My nose is full of what
You call it—'snot!'
Mein Gott, the rickets or the rot,
I always vant an English rose—
And this is what I got—Mein Gott"

Prodding my bottom on the word 'this' and going into great ha-ha-has. The tune was a version of the Horst Wessel song and I think it was originally taking the mickey out of either Hitler or the Jews. I don't know how long Norman Drake had stood up by the side of the house watching us. He was covered in dried blood and carrying a pair of water skis on his shoulder.

"I thay!" he was lisping, through the gaps in his teeth.

"Come in!"

"Come on down!"

"Is thith Caroline Latimer's home ... ?"

There was some confusion at first. He was sat down in the shade of the codlin apple tree and given a drink. It appeared that he had been with Weenie and had got involved in some kind of accident on the river. "They've got her," he kept saying.

"Who did this to you?" asked our pretty neighbour. "Not muggers, I hope, not in Guildford?"

"The police," he said.

"What about the police?" asked C.H.

"They've got her!" the poor man exclaimed.

"Oh, splendid," said C.H. "Take him up to the bathroom, Issy. Now what was I saying." And as I led Norman Drake up the garden C.H. was saying: "Roses! That's what I shall ask him about. Nobody ever asks the Prime Minister about his garden. Once you get 'em off politics ministers say quite useful things ..."

There was no real alarm in the air. The police were already there. As C.H. says, in this country the police do work for us—in Russia they work for the public. There is a sinister difference, if you are a magistrate, as I am, or what C.H. calls a constitutional person as he certainly is. His mother was a Dawson, related to Lord Dawson of Penn, King George the Fifth's surgeon, and C.H. is in line for a title if he lives longer than some distant cousin in Canada. This, principally, is why we became vegetarians. Meanwhile we regard him as Sir Charles Latimer and he has already got an OBE. As for the drama ... The permanent erection is quite old hat. Eskimos get it right through their hibernation period, my friend Phillip Coulson told me. He is now health officer for Godalming, but he once ran a hospital in Newfoundland. St Johns.

"It's a disease of the lower orders," he said. "It's like communism. They spend their lives sitting over holes in the ice and if you give them anything better—catch something they didn't expect—they don't know what the hell to do with it." He said what happens to the permanently hard male organ is that it finally sloughs off. It becomes nothing, like a rotted carrot. It is as much a killer as gangrene or cancer.

Nobody ever discovered the truth about the origins of Weenie's red lettuce plague. While it was a bandit vegetable creating sexual havoc its properties were officially denied; but as soon as it was harnessed into tins and jars and juices, the same properties were officially claimed. It gave my autistic daughter something to get her teeth into; made of her a Marie Stopes, a Madam Curie, a heroine of Women's Lib. Our proudest day was when C.H. and I went up to Oxford to watch Weenie receive her honorary degree in the Sheldonian.

"Women dominate on their knees," said the vice chancellor.

"Do they, Rab?" said Caroline. Her picture is in the hall, sweet in cap and ermine-collared gown, holding her favourite chopper. At heart, we autistics never ever lose our basic lunacy. In the outside world it crumbles mountains.

"Inside every liberated woman is a man," I told Weenie, "looking for his slave." "Is there, mummy?" she said. She was holding Katy's hand at the time. We were having dinner at The Blue Boar.

13

Katy sat cowboy style on a bar stool, her knees up, her heels hooked up on the top rungs. She was so angry it wouldn't come out unless it all came out in one blah. It was like wanting to pass water so badly that it would be perilous to take even one step toward the loo. Caroline, taking the next stool in the entrance bar could sense this without hearing one word spoken. Katy's knuckles were white on the telephone grip. By her side was a large brandy and a little stock of roll-ups prepared, one would judge, for this conversation. All she was saying was:

"Yes. I know that. I know that. I know that. Stop telling me what I already know. No. Yes. Shut up a minute. Let me say something. This is our last conversation. I never ever want to see you again as long as I live. I am quite calm, thank you. You tricked me. You are an unmitigated scoundrel and liar. I do mean it. And now you are a murderer. I said murderer and I mean murderer."

Captain Turner came in, spotted Caroline, hurried across and laid a hand on her shoulder. "No luck I'm afraid—"

Caroline without looking at him raised her arm and put her hand across his mouth.

"What I saw in that field by the river this afternoon was the most horrifying and inhuman thing since those pictures of Belsen and Buchenwald. I am not exaggerating."

Andy became riveted, looked at Caroline questioningly. She nodded. This was the girl they were looking for. Policemanlike, Andy checked the doors and escape routes and indicated a pint of wallop to the barmaid before joining in the eavesdropping.

The barmaid, a ladylike girl called Sybil, had already registered the interesting conversation and she pulled a pint for Andy and a glass of whisky for Caroline with the most tacit instruction, not clinking bottles or glasses, as though they had entered in the middle of a television play. A family sat near the door, also listening, since children could be smuggled just inside the entrance. Two old-age pensioners, a man and his wife, sat on a bench seat almost under the telephone, staring, you would think, into their comfortable past.

"Murder is the only word possible. You are a killer of the worst kind. One who does not even look at his victim. Well, you should. You really should. You should see the eyes bulging out and the bared teeth biting on the black tongue."

Andy slid off his stool and urgently beckoned the barmaid out through the other end of the bar, he himself passing out of sight into the next bar where they met.

"Have you got another telephone, miss?"

"Through there. You'll need a coin."

"No, I won't."

Captian Turner found the telephone engaged and pulled a man away from it. "Emergency, sorry—it's murder" The man stepped back and watched as Andy dialled 999.

The man said: "I was already on to 999—my boat's been nicked."

"Fuck your boat, sir," said Andy. "I want the following call traced as quickly as possible," he instructed, having made his preliminary identifications.

Not until Lady Catherine groped for another roll-up did she notice Caroline, who lit it for her. The girl covered the phone for a moment to exclaim: "Hello. Am I glad to see you. I've been searching everywhere. Wait 'till you hear what's happened—" Then, replying to something infuriating on the line: "Liar. I don't believe you. You're too old to change now. You'll just go on killing and killing and killing. Now I know what happened to Bertie and Fred, don't I? Well, don't I? I don't give a monkey's whether they were—what? Oh! I see! and you think that is a justification?"

Andy rejoined the audience and patiently waited, hoping the

call would continue long enough to be traced. He was quite disconcerted when Katy noticed his appearance and gave him a brief, polite smile. Then she said:

"Lust! That's all it is. Lust. It's in your blood. It was in your father's blood and his father's blood. There are little bodies strewn right through the family history. In a halfway civilised state you would be in Broadmoor. All right, tell me, I'm listening."

While Lady Catherine Vesey listened with hard unbelieving eyes, she smoked and drank her brandy and with gestures offered Andy and Caroline a round, which they accepted. Captain Turner found it a curious if not unique situation. Caroline Latimer did not. Her friends had sat through many such conversations she had conducted with her fucking whore of a mother. On the telephone was the only way one could effectively talk frankly with close relations. Caroline had long ago ceased imagining that it was Timothy at the other end of the line. Such satisfying interchanges were possible only with mother, father, brother, sister, husband, wife or lover after a too-long engagement or understanding.

"Rubbish," said Katy at last. "Rubbish rubbish rubbish rubbish rubbish rubbish—" she shouted to drown the rubbish from the other end. Then she said: "I am not hysterical. I am talking to a mass murderer and I am trying to remain rational. You do not have the first idea what agonies you cause. Deafness, blindness, paralysis—not just spots on the liver as you so blandly claim. No, I do not want to continue this conversation either. I just want you to know that I have discovered your foul crime. You may get away with it on earth, but God will hang you. Goodbye. What? Oh, fuck off, daddy!"

Lady Catherine slammed down the receiver and blew smoke into the air. Took a swig of her brandy and choked a little. Then she smiled at Caroline: "Sorry about all that, Caroline,"

"You were marvellous," Caroline told her. "You only swore once in all that time. I wish I could be like that. I swear too fucking much."

Andy finished his beer and then, ungratefully, considering who had paid for it: "Never mind all that, miss—where is he?"

"Mm?" said Katy.

"This is Andy," Caroline explained. "Captain Turner. Sort of police. Special branch. I'm afraid he's on duty."

They shook hands, but Andy would not let go yet: "Where's chummy? Timothy?"

"Oh!" Katy laughed uproariously. "Poor Timothy."

Caroline grew depressed and started squinting a little. She had noticed more and more during this super weekend that people used the term "poor" about somebody either just before or after they died.

Andy gripped Katy's hand more firmly, with just the merest suggestion of torture on her knuckle bones: "Where is he? Where was he phoning from? Don't bother to lie because I shall have the information in two shakes. The call is being traced."

A little bewilderd, Lady Catherine said: "What call? That was daddy. I've got Timothy tied up in the boat."

Andy released her hand and Katy said to Caroline, her voice rising with incredulity; "You should have told me! He's a bit kinky, isn't he, to say the least? He made me tie him up! I mean, I've read about it. I'm not a child. Did you know that he was epileptic? We'd hardly had our picnic when he went racing off into the fields. He felt an attack coming on and didn't want me to see it. They recover on their own, you know. I thought he'd gone for a shit. There's no convenience on the boat. When he came back he was in this awful state, all mud and blood and scratches. 'Tie me up and ring Martin,' he kept saying. Who's Martin?"

"That's his landlord," Caroline said. "A rather nice old queer."

"Ah! I see." A certain amount of understanding dawned in her lovely boyish face. "That might explain Timothy, mightn't it?"

"It might," Caroline agreed.

Captain Turner was depressed; suspicion had faded into something like boredom. It began to look as though Timothy was not chummy after all. Girl-talk rather bored him. Elsie was forever going on about her dry cunt. He smelt his fingers, thinking about it. Sybil lent across to him and whispered something. He said "Duke of whatalow?"

Katy caught it: "That's daddy. He is a beast."

The barmaid said: "The man said whatever you're working on, scrub it."

"All right, all right, all right. Let's do this again, shall we? What's that, whisky and brandy? Bloody wars. This'll be on expenses."

"So anyway," Katy said, "when I tied him up I felt this awful hernia. Do you know he's got a lump in his groin as big as my fist! I told him if he doesn't get it seen to it will strangulate. I did ten months at the Royal Free before I joined the BBC. Is your sister Julia? I remembered afterwards it wasn't her I disliked, it was a girl named Judith. If you've got a title, people think you can't be a communist. If you'd seen this rabbit this afternoon you'd want to hang the landowners. Genocide, that's what I call it. Why does man assume that he is the supreme being? It's the same with badgers. Bertie and Fred were badgers. Lovely old brocks. They say they carry tuberculosis to cows. Why don't they exterminate cows? Badgers don't give milk, you see. No, it's man first, man second, man all the time. Are you a friend of the earth, Caroline?"

Tiredly and without much interest now, Andy said: "You didn't come across a little boy this afternoon?"

"Yes, we did. Two little boys. They were killing this poor rabbit. Finishing it off. 'It's got myxie, miss,' they said. Holding it by the feet and banging its head against a gatepost. Then I saw it properly." Suddenly Lady Kate couldn't go on because she was crying. Caroline held her arm and they both wept for a minute and the new drinks came. The man came back to join his little family by the door.

"We'll have to go home by taxi—I've just organised it. The police say ours is the third boat stolen today. They're after little cabin cruisers now fuel's so dear."

"Oh, Malcolm! What about all our stuff? I told you I didn't want to stop for a drink ..."

"Daddy always told us it was painless, like having gas at the dentist. I was only about seven when myxomatosis was introduced. Painless! 'How did you catch this rabbit?' I asked the boy."

"How old was he?" asked the captain.

"I don't know. 'Jes walked up to it. miss,' he said. 'They can't tell nothing.' Caroline, it was hideous."

"Well, roughly?" asked the captain. "Five? Ten? Fifteen?"

"Ten," said Lady Kate. "One a bit older. To think my father has massacred nearly half a million acres of rabbit warren in Scotland and Hampshire. Spraying the burrows with his foul genetic disease. How would we feel getting sprayed with VD? All our babies born blind? They never ate more than ten percent of crops. Any ecologist will tell you that. Well, aren't they entitled to it?"

"Did you leave your friend Timothy alone with the boys at any stage?" asked Andrew Turner, doggedly.

"Why?" asked Katy.

"Did you? Never mind why."

Katy turned to Caroline: "Has something happened?"

Caroline said: "We think Timothy may have done something rather naughty."

"Done what?"

Caroline said: "I'm not allowed to say."

"He's been with me all the afternoon. Tied up with mooring rope ever since he had his fit. I brought that boat all the way from Cox's Lock single-handed. I sank a canoe!"

Andy said: "What was his manner when he was tied up?"

Lady Catherine said "Rather alarming. He kept groaning and trying to touch himself. You know. I think he wanted me to do something. I pretended I didn't understand. Luckily the boat was a full-time job."

Andrew said: "Did all this start after he had eaten the salad?"

"Yes. We had our picnic on the bank when we got back from our walk. That was when we saw the boys killing the rabbit."

"May I ask you a personal question?" said the captain; going straight on: "After Timothy had eaten the salad did he try to fondle you? Sexually, I mean?"

"Do I have to answer that?" asked Lady Catherine.

"Yes," Caroline told her.

"Can I have another drink, then? Not brandy. Pint of mixed."

Andy ordered more drinks from Sybil the barmaid, who was impatient to hear the answer and leaned in all the time.

"Where's our boat, daddy?" a child kept repeating.

"I'm waiting," said Andy. "You can whisper if you like."

"If you must know," said Lady Catherine, "no, he didn't."

"He didn't?"

"He didn't touch me. I mean you would think on a hot day like this dressed in nothing, practically, something would happen, wouldn't you? Well, wouldn't you?"

Andy said: "I thought you said after he was tied up he wanted you to touch him?"

Caroline said: "That is not quite the same thing."

Katy said: "And he kept calling me 'young chap' and 'little fellow'. As a sort of joke, I suppose. Once or twice he rubbed against my bottom but I wasn't having that."

The policeman said: "What was Timothy like with the boys?"

"All over them," said Katy. When he started cutting the stomach open to show us the liver Timothy got quite excited. I had to drag him away."

Andy said: "Who cut whose stomach open?"

"The boy, the big boy, knew all about myxomatosis. He wanted to show us the rabbit's liver. Apparently they have spots on." She began to break down again and Caroline passed her a pint mug of mixed. Lady Catherine was already three parts sloshed.

"Then you went back and had your picnic, leaving the boys doing a post-mortem on the dead rabbit?"

"Ssssh!" said Katy. She motioned towards the family by the door where a good deal of crying and wailing was going on.

"Won't we ever see our boat again?" asked a small girl. "I've told you. It's been stolen."

"Their boat's been stolen," Andy told Katy.

"Thass rotten. Issa rotten day. I say!" She called to the family and tried to unhook her heels from her stool but toppled it;

Andy managed to catch her. She thanked him, coolly, and went across to the family. "Have you loss your boat?" The man said: "Yes. And we're not the only ones." Lady Catherine said: "How much did it coss?" "Eight hundred pounds, miss. It was second hand." She said: "Issit sured?" The wife said: "Of course not. Malcolm doesn't do things like that. Not until it's too late."

Lady Catherine Vesey took out a folded cheque book from the back pocket of her jeans and spread it on their table, pushing aside bottles and glasses. "S'pensomebody."

The man gave her a pen and said: "You can't do this, miss. You don't even know us!"

Katy considered this, then said: "Washaname?"

The man said: "Mr Lardner."

Captain Andrew Turner had joined the party and he laid a restraining hand on Lady Catherine's shoulder. "Now look here—" Caroline again placed her hand over his mouth.

"Mislarner," said Katy. Laboriously she began to write.

Andy said to Caroline: "Where's that boat?"

"I'll show you," said Caroline. To Katy, she said: "Come back to the boat when you've finished—okay?"

"'Kay," said Katy. To the family she said: "Don't worry. Thish dirty money. My father's. Capitalish swine. Make thousan' poun'. Thing's gonnup." She tore out the cheque very carefully indeed so as not to rip it, then gave it to the man. "Shcoll!"

"Thank you very much indeed," said Mr Lardner.

The wife and the children stared at the girl, wide-eyed. Watched her go back to the bar, empty three glasses into her mouth, pick up shoes and handbag and cross the room, crabwise, towards the conservatory bar and the river. She turned at the door and gave the contents of the bar, blurred though they appeared, a little queen-like wave as a goodnight blessing.

14

"I say. Excuse me. Petey! Ahoy!"

The motor-sailer was turning in the middle of the river, Petey at the tiller, Sweetie Jenny on the bow watching the bank. Concentrating, Petey called: "Wait a minute!"

"They know where it is," said Caroline.

"There's only one cut and that's the cut. He must have untied himself and pissed off. He must know there's a hue and cry out for him."

"What is it?" Petey now had the craft parellel with the pub lawn.

Caroline called: "Where's that boat? The Micro-Plus?"

"Haven't you found it?" said Petey.

"We thought you'd found it," said Sweetie. "Some men just took it out of the water. I thought your friend had broken down—that's why she was phoning."

Petey said: "It's gone off on a lorry. They had about six boats aboard."

"Bloody crooks! Right under your nose." Andy grumbling.

"There's a police boat moored up there," Petey said, pointing to where *The Jolly Farmer's* marina swelled half across the river.

"Is there?" said Andy. "I'm not surprised." To Caroline, he said: "This is your friend Norman's work. Norman, Nigel Fry and a few bent coppers. Holy tripartite."

"Issay. Where's Timothy?" Lady Katy had appeared. She held onto Andy's leg while she put her shoes on. "Where's boat?"

Caroline said: "It's gone. Stolen. They've taken him with it!"

The captain said: "They wouldn't know he was there if he was tied up in the cabin." Sweetie Jenny called from the boat: "Is that the one that was chloroformed?" Caroline said: "No. It's somebody else." "He must have been fast asleep," said Katy, sobering fast. "Had a lot of wine." Petey called: "Anything I can do to help? 'Fraid I'm blocking the river." Caroline called: "No, it's all right. Thank you very much." Andy called: "How many men?" "Five," said Petey. "Six," said Sweetie. "Sweetie would know," said Petey. Andy called: "We may want your evidence—can you tell me your name and address?" Caroline said: "I've got all that."

Captain Turner gave her a special little smile; from the moment she had said 'I'm not allowed to say' he knew he was onto a winner.

"Goodbye now!" called Sweetie Jenny.

Petey waved.

"Aren't they nice," said Caroline Latimer, sadly. It was like seeing something precious from the real world chugging away out of reach. They waved back once more and Petey peeped his horn, bless him. Caroline had to knuckle her contact lenses.

Katy put her arm around her: "Friends?"

Caroline shook her head.

Katy said: "You're thinking about that rabbit. I keep thinking about that."

"Come back to the bar," the captain suggested. And as they did, passing the river folk returning to their boats, he said: "There's going to be a lovely sunset."

Caroline Latimer, preparing her thesis afterwards, remembered thinking how completely out of character that remark was; unless he too had at some stage eaten the wrong mushroom. It can't be any fun being wanted for murder when murder is your duty to God and the Queen.

There was this very human incident as the girls went back into the hall bar of the pub. Caroline noted it because the stiff-cock phenomenon on the whole lacked humanities. The little boatless family had been on their way out when they saw their benefactress returning and what's more looking sober. Mr

Lardner drew his wife and kids out of sight into the telephone alcove under the hotel stairs until the girls had passed. But then, because God was in his soul and his cock was limp, he touched his wife's cheek, asking her forgiveness, then went after the girls, catching them up as they mounted their stools at the bar and Captain Turner commandeered the bar telephone.

"Here I am, miss," said Mr Lardner. He was holding out the cheque to her.

Puzzled, she said: "What do you want?" Then she said: "Didn't I sign it?"

"Yes, miss. I thought p'raps you'd come to your senses. I mean, reconsidered."

Caroline was looking back towards the family who had now emerged into view and were waiting for the dream to end.

Lady Catherine Vesey waved the cheque away as of no moment; or the last moment, which is less than no moment. She said: "Can I buy you some drinks—what about the children?"

But there was a taxi waiting and they went, all of them, close together, hurrying.

"This is an emergency, Captain Turner—sorry, Angel Face I mean—raise Elsie for me, will you? She might be still servicing Nick and his dog, or she might be interrogating a suspect, or she might be asleep. I've got a talk to her. Give you a minute— take this number." To Sybil, he said: "Wassis number?"

She said: "It's written on there."

He jumped up, suddenly, and to Caroline said: "Give 'em this number. I gotta piss."

He ran out. Caroline took over the phone.

"Do you sell Pils?" Lady Catherine asked Sybil.

"What, birth control pills?"

"No! Oh, my God!" Katy burst into laughter, which caught on with the barmaid and then with the old-age pensioners and with others who were standing and sitting drinking about the place.

"Can I have a bit of quiet?" asked Caroline, covering her unemployed ear.

"Didn't you hear what she said?" asked Katy.

"Yes, we'll be waiting for your call," Caroline told Sycamore, efficiently. Soon, she would be getting fucked by dogs, she could feel it in her bones.

"I hate people saying piss and fuck and things like that," Lady Catherine Vesey confessed to Caroline before the captain came back. "Do you mind dropping him a hint?"

"It doesn't mean anything, you know, not these days."

"I don't care if it means anything or not, Caroline." She accepted her lager and gave Caroline a whisky and put a pint up for the policeman. She said, carefully: "It is not shliv, shliverous—oh, fuck, chivalrous—for a gentleman to swear in front of ladies. It is not a compliment to fenilimility—femilimity."

The barmaid, who had not quite stopped laughing at the pills joke now started heaving at the new one and soon everybody was laughing again.

"Issnice here," said Katy. She hooked her heels up again like a cowboy. Captain Andrew Turner came back and Katy said: "Don't tell him what I said. Fuck it, eh?"

"All right," said Caroline. It was the beginning; their first mutual corruption.

"This mine?" said Andy. "Cheers!" And soon, when he had wiped his mouth, he said: "Don't worry. Soon have Timothy back."

"Why don't you just set up a road block?" Katy asked. "One would have thought a lorry-load of stolen cabin cruisers pretty easy to find."

"That would blow our cover," said Caroline Latimer. She gave Andy the superior, myopic stare she gave outwitted bankrupts.

He nodded his approval as the telephone buzzed. "It's for me," he told Sybil.

"Yes, I know. It's probably Elsie," she said. It was Elsie.

"Elsie? Andy. Never mind Angel Face, we're going to drop all that kids' stuff. Listen, where are you? What the hell are you doing at home? Oh, come on. You're always going home. You can sleep tomorrow, it's the Queen's birthday. What is it, then? Well, that'll do. Now what have you done with chummy?

Drake. I need him. Where did he go? Well, you *should* know. They've knocked off half a dozen boats and Timothy's in one of 'em tied up. Tied up! I don't know any more than you do. We've got to find him and fast. You heard the news? About those boys? Well then. If the police find out, we've had it."

Conversation began to rise to cover what appeared to be a compromising and private conversation. Lady Catherine Vesey leaned closer to Caroline.

"I thought he *was* the police?"

"Special branch," Caroline told her.

"What does he mean about those boys?" asked Katy.

"I can't tell you here. You'll have to wait."

"What naughty thing did Timothy do?"

"Ssssh."

"What have you done with Crouch? I see. What have you done with the stuff you took out of Miss Latimer's fridge? Good. See you get a good price. Here's your job, then. Nick and Tiger are all right, are they? Good girl. All right, don't go on. Get Nick to take Harry, Fred and George and pick up Nigel Fry. Make him tell 'em where the boats are. Don't bruise him. Put him in the spin drier. We haven't got time to mess about. When you've located this Timothy—" then aside to the girls: "What's his moniker?"

"Timothy Tite" Caroline said, adding: "He's a hospital administrator, lives at—"

"Just a minute, just a minute. Elsie, when you've located this Timothy Tite don't untie him until you've sussed him out. He may want cunt, he may want a bum—I'm not asking you to! For Christ's sake, we're short-handed, it doesn't hurt you to turn the other cheek in an emergency. Oh, balls, Elsie, there's jar and jars of the bloody stuff in our stores—what? I do not know, I have not asked her. All right, hang on. Miss Latimer—Caroline. Elsie's overworked. She really is overworked. That bloody lettuce is getting everywhere and we're short-staffed—it's all pricks and no cunts. Will you sign the Sycamore work contract? I'll give you a clue—if you don't you're going to be shot. I mean, it's not me. I like you. We haven't got time to be

selective. If Timothy's little caper was brought home to us—
and I do mean you, Caroline—it could bring down the
government. What about it? Elsie's waiting."

Caroline Latimer looked at her empty glass. She had so far
managed to avoid buying a round of drinks but it was her turn
plus. She said: "With certain provisos. Are drinks on
expenses?"

"She says yes—I'll get her to sign it now. There's somebody
else here, too." he looked with friendly inquiry at Lady
Catherine Vesey. "Would you be interested in social work?"

Katy was genuinely bewildered. "Well, yes. Well, I don't
know. Could I combine it with my BBC research job?"

"She says yes," the captain told the phone. "That's two more
mobile fucks if we want them. Then you've got Margery, once
she's got over Dobbin. In another couple of weeks we shall be
getting wanking machines up from Ding Dong. They take a
dozen at a time. The Tripods walk in like cows for milking.
These new machines have got tits and arses, something to grip,
all at body temperature. Come Christmas, you'll be able to sit
on it again. How's your mum and dad? Good. And given them
mine. Goodnight, love, God bless."

He hung up and turned to the bar. "She's nice, really, old
Elsie. Oh God, I meant to warn her about Timothy."

"What's that tune that Lauren Bacall sings in *To Have and
Have Not*? Caroline asked. "I think that's it on the tape. Will
you have a drink with me, now, Katy?"

"Then I'll have to go." Katy had seen the red light. Out of all
the confusions of the day, this now was the one definite thing in
her mind to get away.

Captain Andrew Turner had been carried away with his
harrassing staff problems and the drink, but now he realised
from Caroline's oblique behaviour that he had said too much,
perhaps. Familiarity had coarsened Sycamore's terms of
reference beyond even the most progressive conventions. Fuck
and cunt and cock and prick and every variety and position and
extremity of sexual intercourse and masturbation were to the
members of Sycamore like plant names in a seed shop.
Coarsened by use, the obscenity calendar is useless.

Katy said: "I think I'll just have a tonic water, Caroline."

Andy finished his drink and got up; he was really dead beat. From his pocket he took a roll of recruitment contracts and peeled off two. "Take these. Think about it. Pay's good and there's lot's of fun. You're saving men's lives very often—well, you know that, Caroline. Dobbin only cut his cock off because he thought you didn't care."

Caroline said: "That was very remiss of me." To Lady Catherine, she explained: 'He bled to death in the bath."

"I am sorry. Were you close?"

"He's not the only one," said the captain. Then he pointed at them, much like the Kitchener poster: "You can save them!" He prepared to leave them. "Right then. I promised my missis I'd be home at eight. I'm helping her with her A-levels. Anybody want dropping? I'm going to—"

"No, thank you!" said Caroline and Catherine together.

"To Wimbledon," he finished.

"Thanks awfully," said Caroline. "I'm home already—I live in Guildford." "And I'm going to the palace," said Lady Catherine. "I'm going right past Crystal Palace," Andy said. "Oh. No, not that one. I'll be perfectly all right," said Catherine. "You could stay with me tonight?" Caroline offered. "I have to be in the law courts in the morning. We could go up together on the eight-five." "Super," said Lady Catherine Vesey. "Goodnight, then," said Andy. "I'll be in touch. Got your gun, have you, Caroline?" She said: "Yes, thank you." He said: "Shoot anybody who gets in your way, but let me know before the freightliner leaves for Ding Dong. We collect bodies and stiff pricks all over London and the Home Counties. Here, here's my card." He gave her a card and with a final, "Charah!" Captain Andrew Turner of Sycamore left *The Jolly Farmer*.

They drank for a moment in relieved silence, then Caroline Latimer said: "I suppose I ought to fill you in. Put you in the picture."

Katy said, quickly: "I think it might be safer if you didn't, Caroline. I'm a bit of a chatterbox once I start. If you don't mind." Then she leavened the refusal with a lovely boyish smile: "But I will stay with you tonight if it's perfectly all right with your parents."

That smile of Katy's did something to Caroline Latimer that nothing had done since Warren Morgan looked at her in the lecture hall at Ox. Her production machine jammed up with a great scream of tortured cunning. She would willingly stay with Catherine and be her slave. She was in love with her, romantically and physically and intellectually. Caroline wanted to sleep with Lady Catherine and fuck her and be fucked by her. If only they could eat the red lettuce, that piece she had hidden in her knicker leg for C. H. Latimer. And if only they could grow beautiful red-, white- and blue-tinged horns for each other and rest them in each other's own tender tissue.

"Who is Dobbin?" Catherine spoke gently, below the hall bar's threshold of hearing, as though joining Caroline after a mutual communion of spirit.

"A nice policeman. His mother lives in Stevenage."

"Why did he mutilate himself?"

Caroline Latimer gathered the facts and spoke concisely. "You saw the rabbit, Katy. I saw the man."

The two women looked deeply into each other's eyes. From Lady Catherine Vesey's cowboy saddle, the Official Receiver's examiner was silhouetted soft as a virginal schoolmarm in the fragment of promised sunset beyond Godalming.

15

The sun set several more lovely times that Sunday night of that same super weekend. It set from the top, into the mountains of cloud, turning them gold. It set in the middle like a beautiful cheese set in beautiful streaky bacon. It finally hung like a scarlet, incandescent hot-air balloon with a frilly-knicker bottom that was really a part of the slate-grey cloud. A sharply defined globe against a void. No beam came from it, the summer sky had died, the hot day gone, only this one ember left, pulled down by ropes to form a little corrugation along the bottom. A showman's most grandiloquent dream of an eye-catching idea which caught very few eyes being free. Lady Catherine Vesey saw it over Caroline Latimer's shoulder as they climbed towards the Cathedral of the Holy Spirit on Stag Hill.

"Why did your friend Andy calls us a couple of mobile fucks?" Katy asked.

Caroline was holding Katy's arm: "First you say you'd rather not know anything, then you keep asking questions."

"Yes. Well, I'm sorry. I don't want to know. Look at that sunset."

They stopped and admired it together, like lovers, the red light in their faces. In seconds the hot-air balloon became a parachute and then a flying saucer and then a sliver and then nothing. They continued their way under the precipice of the new cathedral.

"Is there anyone home?" asked Katy. Then she said: "I'm mad. I was thinking you lived here."

"This is the cathedral."

"Yes, I realize that. It was consecrated in 1961. HRH was

here. You get so conditioned to enormous erections you expect everybody to live in them. Did I say something funny?"

Caroline Latimer shook her head, but her shoulders quaked for a moment.

"Mind you," said Katy, "I live in a right old rabbit warren in Chelsea. Flatlets. We call it the warren. It's matey, though. I like that, don't you?"

Caroline stopped by the door of the Lady Chapel and put her fingers on Katy's cheeks, facing her, looking up at her. She said: "I love you, Katy." This was really why she had come the cathedral way home. She wished to sanctify that one profession of her love for somebody who was not bleeding Warren Morgan the fucking solicitor. She wanted it to be one up on him, above the touching of toes in the sharp end of a boat.

"I'll pretend you didn't say that," said Katy.

"One can pretend," Caroline Latimer whispered. There was a certain mutual acceptance of the situation in this interchange. It released them from the need to be serious and they sat on some sacred statuary and lit up smokes.

"Show me where you live, Caroline."

Caroline pointed south-west, then moved it a little. "Onslow," she said. "A semi-detached with a fish pond and a fucking peacock. Or at least, there will be. Daddy is impotent. That's C. H. Latimer Exactly, broadcaster and journalist. Vegetarian, dietician, all that. Quite nice. Bit useless."

"Not a murdering beast like my father. Though of course I love him really. You know."

"Yes, I do mine" said Caroline. "Well, you have to."

"Let me put my arm around you," said Lady Catherine. "You look cold." And when she had, she said: "Are you a prostitute, Caroline?"

Caroline said: "No. I'm an Official Receiver's examiner in the Thomas More building at the Royal Courts of Justice in the Strand."

"Oh, I see," said Katy. "I hope you didn't mind me asking. I've been listening to everything and I thought I'd got it all worked out. I thought perhaps your friend Captain—whatsit—"

Caroline said: "Turner."

"Yes, Turner. Was a pimp. Well, on a nice big scale, running a call-girl service or something. You remember when he was talking to someone called Elsie? Mobile fucks and servicing people and wanking machines, tits and arses, something to grip. It all sounded terribly, well, efficient, industrial—commercial. Where does Timothy fit in?"

Caroline had been rubbing her cheek against Katy's breast through the short woollen jumper, her mind pleasantly emptying. She said: "Will you sleep with me, Katy?"

"This stone is hurting my bum," said Lady Catherine.

"It's been a really lovely summer," said Caroline Latimer.

"Super."

"I don't love anybody but you," said Caroline Latimer.

"Bonny's at sea," said Lady Catherine Vesey.

A soft sell had been clinched into a soft deal.

16

A ladylike scream came from the direction of Caroline's house as they reached it. Street lights had turned dusk into darkness and the blue and coloured flickering of television was visible through curtains and blinds as they passed. The Latimer house was in darkness apart from one upstairs front bedroom.

"Listen," Caroline requested. The scream came again, a cultured sound of informed terror or anger; as though, if rape, it was too tight rather than too much. "It sound like mummy," said Caroline.

"Gosh," said Katy. "Do they quarrel?"

"Not in the bedroom," Caroline Latimer told her new sweetheart. "There's nothing to quarrel about."

As she was organising a key in the yale lock of the front door she said: "Katy …"

"Yes?"

"Are you with me all the way?"

Lady Catherine Vesey hesitated only momentarily. The question could relate to making love in bed or it could relate to screams and wanking machines. She said: "Yes."

The two girls entered into the dark hall of the semi-detached house where the rubber plant stood.

Caroline said: "Put your luggage down here and come with me. Don't worry, I've got my gun."

"There's a lot of luggage here already," said Lady Katy. There was an unaccustomed amount of bags and parcels and tennis racquets, with a pair of water-skis taller than the stair bannister. "Oh fuck. I expect Julia's turned up with her BB twit." Katy's only luggage was a black BEA air-travel case with her name in the Perspex window with an address at The Cloisters, SW3. Caroline had her parasol and her gun bag.

Caroline said: "You go to the bathroom and I'll see what's happening to Isobel. That's her name."

"I though *you* wanted the bathroom?" said Katy.

"Yes, but I want a fucking good evacuation and the lot. One's inclined to bottle it up on the river, I find. Run some hot water if you like and we'll take a bath together afterwards. Lots of foam and some of daddy's Scotch. There are some yellow ducks we can float. Follow me."

They went up the stairs, Caroline switching on lights inside saints on alabaster plinths which glowed on red tapestry wallpaper.

"Why is everybody in bed so early?" asked Lady Catherine.

"They're trying to fuck, I expect. After a time one finds oneself dedicated to one's shortcomings. The mind positively boggles. You go in there, darling."

The word slipped out and held them, for a second, motionless; they embraced spontaneously. The front bedroom door opened and C. H. Latimer peered out. Inquisitively he watched the two women kissing passionately. He could see the back of Lady Catherine Vesey's short fair bobbed hair and his daughter's arms around her, one hand running over the curvature of the stranger's bottom, the other holding a gun across her shoulders.

"Is that you, Weenie?" asked C. H. Latimer.

"Who is it?" called Isobel's voice within the bedroom.

"I think it's Weenie."

"I love you," Caroline told Catherine.

"I know you do," said Katy.

"Weenie?" said C. H. Latimer.

"Oh do shut up, daddy, when we're in the middle of something."

But now it was spoiled and they gave him peripheral attention. "This is my father, C. H. Latimer Exactly. Daddy, this is Catherine Vesey."

"Good God," said C. H. Latimer. "Is it still absolutely true your father's having to kill all his pines now?" He had the yellowing, dried, feathered look of a very old penguin, loped with a commuter's gait, arms heavy with wrist watches.

Katy said: "I expect so. Must pee."

"What a ripping girl, Weenie." C. H. Latimer watched her scrabble for the bathroom, holding her crutch. Then, looking at his daugher. "Your friend Norman's been telling us everything."

"Norman Drake?"

Caroline's father indicated his bedroom: "He's in rather a bad way. Cut up. No wonder. Are you perfectly all right? Come in."

Caroline Latimer entered her parents' Austin Suite room and found Norman Drake sitting up in bed getting spoonfed by her mother.

"We're giving him some bran mash," her father explained. "His front teeth have gone."

Norman's potato face looked mashed and he had been crying. He looked at Caroline with the spoon in his mouth, the mash dribbling on his chin, his eyes red but pleased to see her.

"Sam's dead," were his first intelligible words, connecting his condition not with his own suffering but Sam's and warming her heart toward him again.

"Hello, darling," said Isobel, without looking round.

"Hello, mummy." Caroline kissed the back of her mother's neck and pressed her shoulder gratefully for looking after her friend. Their middle-class hate for each other was entirely atavistic, a third-person telephonic thing.

"What about Nigel Fry?" asked Caroline. "They were going to put him in a spin dryer if he wouldn't tell them where the boats are."

"Yeth, I know. Thorry about my teeth. They put *me* in the thpin dryer. Different chaps. They thought I was Nigel. Nigel had gone to Sunbury to visit Tham. Vithit Tham. Oh thyit!"

Caroline leaned over and wiped his chin. "Don't cry, darling. So they put you in the spin dryer as well. You poor thing. What about Tim? What about the boats?"

"I'll tell her," Isobel said. "Don't keep asking him questions, darling. The boats were sunk."

"Oh my god!" cried Caroline.

"What's the trouble?" asked Lady Catherine, coming in.

"Timothy's drowned!" said Caroline.

"No he's not," said her mother.

"They always sink stolen craft," C. H. Latimer explained to Katy. "It's the best way to hide them. Tied together, submerged, in a gravel workings at Staines. They come to no harm. Plastic, most of them. They pull 'em out and clean 'em up as they want them. Rather neat."

"But what about Timothy?" asked Katy.

"He was lucky," Isobel said. "He was in a bubble."

"Of course he was in a bubble," said Caroline. "He's got pull. He's the bishops' fucking bum boy."

"Weenie!" said her father.

"Listen." Isobel Latimer was leaning closer to the invalid. "He's trying to say something. Lady Vesey—I believe it's for you." Isobel made way for Katy near Norman's damaged mouth.

Caroline whispered to her parents: "What's happened to his hands?" Norman's hands had been heavily bandaged with oatmeal crepe around the palms.

Her mother said: "He escaped on water skis. All the way from Hampton to Sunbury between the locks."

"Nigel's sea scouts in a speedboat," explained her father. "He carried the skis all the way here. They cost a lot of money."

"What *about* my father?" Katy was asking Norman.

"Your father is Big Tree!" Norman hissed.

Caroline said: "I don't believe it. Lord Waterlow head of Sycamore? He's president of the Wild Fowl Trust isn't he?"

"He's in everything up to his neck," Katy said. "He's always been mixed up with the Secret Service. He was in Helsinki when the Russians moved into Hungary in 1956. Or was it '57?"

"Suez '56, I believe, Lady Catherine," said C. H. Latimer.

"Oh yes, and Suez," said Katy. "Daddy happened to be in Beirut. I mean, I believe it instantly. What is Big Tree? Is that Andy's boss?"

"Not any more," said Norman. He was sitting up now, clutching at Katy's shoulder, as if gasping his last words. "The

159

government are cutting back. Sycamore is trying to form a junta. Big meeting tomorrow night at the Royal Free—Hampstead. You must contact your father, Katy. Now! Tell Big Tree!"

Norman Drake sank back, exhausted. Caroline took over from her new friend and lover, stroked his forehead. She said, softly: "He's had a rotten day. Dragged away in the middle of an orgasm."

Her mother said, apologetically: "I had to undress him."

"That's all right, mummy."

Katy said: "What's he saying now?"

Caroline listened at Norman's bruised lips; his eyes were closed. "It sounds like—yes, it is—Jacobski. Dobbin mentioned him. He's the Krasniy Latouk expert from Russia."

Her father said: "I'd like to find out more about that. I could do with something like that myself. Mind you, celery was all the rage at one time."

"Then it was oysters," her mother remembered. She added about the invalid: "Norman hasn't had any lettuce, has he? I mean his dick was quite limp. Firm but limp."

And Lady Catherine Vesey said: "May I use your telephone, Mr Latimer ...?"

C. H.'s complaint has vanished. I have to record an extraordinary success which, although it coincides with the girls visiting us last night, has nothing whatever to do with their strange red lettuce. I am sure nobody in Sycamore would believe this, judging from Weenie's account of that lurid organisation, but I know, since I was there as the receiving party, so to speak, that C. H's triumph was not vegetable but animal. Partly the dentist's wife, Christine, our next-door neighbour, and partly their peacock. It must have been five o'clock in the morning, our bedroom window opened wide to the summer's night, and we were suddenly staring at each other across the bed.

"What on earth was that?" I said.

"It was Christine?" said my husband. "Weenie heard it. You remember when they first got here—she thought it was you—oh my God!" There it was again, a desperate piercing scream thrust into the night on the moment of some fearful torture. Of course they had to get rid of the damn bird quite

quickly; a dentist operating in his own front room can't afford screams like that. We were going to get a peacock ourselves, keeping up with the Jones's, but what a blessing we didn't! Now the point is, we didn't know it was the peacock at first. C. H. thought it was Christine's newest orgasmic cry. The effect on him was remarkable. No need to wait for Chinese students or red lettuce. I couldn't believe it. It's been almost five years.

"C. H.! What are you doing? C. H. What are you doing! Charley! Charley!" "Gojormarvellous!" he kept panting, his head, body, hands all burrowing into me like a badger. Later, we got the whole thing on tape, peacock and all—he won't waste anything, not even a geranium—and he's approaching the BBC with it next week. Well, I don't mind; I've got used to sharing my life with the documentary world. Weenie is her autistic mother over again.

17

Caroline Latimer's textbook, *The Redundant Cock*, was illustrated for the most part with photos and video excerpts from the red lettuce concert of fucking, buggery and automated masturbation taking place on this hot night in July in the Edith Cavell electric lecture hall. Her prefatory exposition was generously peppered with acknowledgments to Dr Jacob Jacobski's disarming lecture delivered on the same occasion.

He sat, a little dwarf of a man, naked apart from his heavy-rimmed glasses with his short, stubby, stiff prick either in his hand or sheltered by the steeple his fingers made when he touched the tips together to mark the various painful stages in the descent of man into rabbit.

"You will notice, laties and gentamen, I haf no blacking board and no chalk to draw cocks. What I haf to show you tonight is here in my hand. Ding dong, ding dong—" he tapped his knob to and fro "—do not be afraid of it and it will not hurt you. Remember this. Your cock, or prick, or john or whateffer you haf familiar terms for it, is bigger up here in your brain box than in your hants or your laties hants. Pull him out often, get to know him, make a fren of him. You sir, in the front row, haf you got him strap up in chains and hin away in the darkness? Take him out of captivity sir, wafe him about, be prout of him, like me. Ding dong, ding dong. Everybody take out your cock like me. Take him out of your trousers and presto—he will come out off your brain box. If you are shy, get the latie next to you to take him out. Here tonight we are all in the same kettle of fish with the red lettuce stiff-cock syndrome. About this I will carry on furthermore with demonstrations with real life people like ourselfs once I see—I say once I see and not before—all your stiff cocks standing up, ding dong, ding dong, ding dong, without fear or fafour and no guilt in the brainbox. Thank you, laties, thank you, sir—you see, it is a big one. Everybody clap. That's right. A big han for a big prick ..."

The lights in the hall were discreetly dimmed while the afflicted unzipped their organs and let them stand free in their laps. A single spotlight fell on a young constable who stood, fully dressed, but with his erection standing out naked as an example, and sang in a rather touching tenor voice, Oh God our help in ages past, Our hope for years to come.

"It's rather good, isn't it?" Captain Andrew Turner had appeared behind Caroline's group and was pulling a chair in between her and Lady Catherine. "Mind you, the old boy's a bit of a fake. His cock is plastic. I saw it hanging in his dressing room in Leeds ..."

"We are the mercenaries, fuck and fight and kill for berries, win or lose we can't do more, we are the sons of SY – CA – MORE!" Hooray, hooray, hooray, was the cry. The girls exchanged nervous glances. Until now they had believed themselves in the hands of proper soldiers and policemen, officers of the state and therefore relatively safe. Lady Catherine and Caroline held hands and this seemed to anger Captain Turner. He pulled them roughly apart. "This is what I mean. This is why you've got to go, my lady. There's no room for personal relations. You've got to be ready to kill your mother. Miss Latimer knows that. What is our leader? One, two, three—"

"BIG TREE!" came the chanted reply.

Martin Pushkin came hurrying with his little steps from a hospital elevator, one hand behind him on his bottom, his painted woman's face searching the crowd until he saw Andy.

"Captain Turner? Captain Turner? I'm sorry to interrupt—don't look at me like that, then, I've done my best, given my bloody all I would say, in public too. Here, Captain, what *are* you going to do with Timothy Tite? My friend he's worried to death! I've been sitting up there a solid hour holding his winkle. Oh, it is a size! After all these months flirting and then boom! You've got to talk to him. He thinks he's going to be put

165

to sleep! I said: 'You're not a dog, you're a human being, Timothy! You've got rights! I told him.' Well, I mean, they're like animals, aren't they? You've got to give them reassurance—Oh! Lady Catherine! I didn't notice you stood there! Excuse me, Captain. Oh, I am relieve to see you, dear. Relieved, I mean. What happened? What in God's name happened, your ladyship?" Now he recognised Caroline. "Oh, it's you. Well, he needs his friends around him now, whoever they are, but for gawd's sake don't bend down or he'll be up you like a ferret after a rabbit—pardon my imagery. What happened after you got on the boat, Catherine? He didn't rape you, did he? Or anything like that?"

"This is Martin," Caroline Latimer explained to her condemned lovely lover.

Martin Pushkin snapped at her: "You don't have to introduce us. Lady Catherine Vesey and myself are old friends. You know, Katy, I'm the one you talk to on the phone and book the table at Keats and so forth."

Katy was only partially enlightened and Martin prodded her bosom with his finger: "You know, we was talking Sunday morning—the day it happened. My dinner was burning. I've got your picture framed in the powder room. Out of *Country Life* when you was getting engaged to Lord Whatsit. Still, we mustn't discuss that now, eh? Water under the bridge if you'll excuse the pun, knowing the commander—"

"Break it up, sir—madam—sir, I mean," said Andy. "We're waiting to move off."

Martin unwisely brushed the captain off without even looking at him, dabbing backward with his soft hand. "Do go away a minute." And to Katy: "How was the funeral? I saw a bit of it on telly. Very impressive, I thought. I suppose all the lands and the house will come to your dad now. Lovely place! Lovely! They did a walk round on Nationwide. He was your grandad, wasn't he? Look, don't keep rubbing my back, I can't stand that." Andy was trying to put a white chalk cross for destruction on Martin's one-piece suit. Only the coincidence of Elsie Thompson entering from the street at that moment saved the old queen from getting chopped down.

18

In came Big Tree, waving all his branches. Lord Jamie, Duke of Waterlow. His life had been devoted to landowning; to stopping the spread of anything which might endanger it, be it wealth or rabbits. With him was a public relations woman, Scottish, astute, her long nose atwitch for anything down-market. It twitched at the sight and sound and smell of Sycamore in the hospital buffet. The Duke, a big man with small, untrustworthy features, was rather embarrassed to find them there—he had come for the lecture. Captain Turner brought his hand from a last placating feel of Elsie straight up into a salute.

"Big Tree! Sar!"

"Yes, yes, good evening, Turner. At ease, please. I hoped you'd be well away by now. You'll be glad to know we are ending the Ding Dong operation at last. In fact it has ended."

"No, sir. Excuse me, sir. You can't do that. We have a full train leaving Paddington at nine sharp."

"It has been cancelled, Turner—"

"No, sir! Impossible, sir!"

"It is not impossible, Turner, it is done—Katy! What the devil are you doing here? This is my daughter Catherine," he told his companion. "This is Margaret Boyd. Margaret is going to promote the red lettuce for its true function. Animal feeding. You'll be glad to know, Katy, we're bringing the rabbits back. Rabbit and goat, they've discovered, yield more protein per feed unit than any other beast. You'll excuse us now—"

Captain Turner held him by the arm: "Just a moment, sir.

That's all very well. What about all the stiff pricks? You can't just leave 'em. It would be inhuman."

Margaret Boyd removed Andy's hand from her new boss's arm. "Have no fear, Captain. There'll be no more eating of the lettuce by humans. We have already developed a new strain which is, I assure you, very unpalatable indeed."

Andy said: "I don't care about that. We must have that train sir. I've got hundreds of stiff cocks waiting, chronic and acute. Literally hundreds. Some of them in that lecture hall getting conned—rehabilitated."

"He's right, daddy. Timothy cost me a thousand pounds conscience money. I had to tie him up. There were some missing boys—didn't you hear about it? Luckily they had simply stolen a boat and skedaddled. God gave me the bill—he must have known the possibilities. That was when I phoned you."

"Good God, child," said the Duke, "I thought you were on about rabbits. Now you get out of this business. Sycamore is no place for the quality. Choose something more befitting a lady of the realm."

Margaret Boyd put in: "Friends of Multiple Sclerosis is very good, your lordship. As we say in our promotion, you are working with people who don't mind being pushed around. It's a little joke, the noo!"

It did not sound like a joke to the mercenary. Andy had seen many ideologies put into cans and sold at a profit. He looked around for help and inspiration.

Caroline Latimer was deep in shallow conversation with a poetic young man in fawn Donegal tweeds decked, in an old-fashioned, legal manner with a spotted bow tie and matching top hankie. Andy Turner hovered on the fringe of what was in fact a passionate reunion.

"And you know the Farmers have split up? Amy and Dick?" Warren Morgan speaking.

"Really?" This had always been the lurid extent of their intercourse. The continuing newsreel of the rest of their Oxford years. She added: "The mind positively boggles.

Though I must say it boggles less about some people. Hello, Andy. This is Warren Morgan. Inter-action, Civil Rights, Amnesty International and so on. I'm taking Amy's house on a bankruptcy repossession order."

Warren said: "That's interesting. What's the statutory period now? After the deed of gift?"

Andy Turner grew gloomy. Many of the people around the hospital foyer bore the stamp of armed secret service men. There was going to be a compulsory demobilisation of Sycamore and blood would flow. "I want you to come with me—"

She said: "Just a moment, Andy. Three years, Warren. Any gift made by a bankrupt during that period has to be returned. Quite embarrassing sometimes as you may imagine. This chap was an old lover of Amy's. Maurice Bernard Rayner? Haberdashers and Christ's. He went on to invent those dog-shit crystals, Antifoul. Unfortunately children started eating them and the bottom fell out—oh."

Andy was pressing his gun hard into her back. "This way."

"Bye Warren," said Caroline Latimer as she was taken through the crowd.

"Bye, Caroline," called the fucking solicitor.

Outside the hospital, the basement reception area, Sycamore ambulances, morgue vans and armoured trucks had been surrounded by Special Air Service regulars.

"Captain Turner!" cried some distant military voice.

"Run," Andy directed.

Together the girl and the man trotted up the ramp into Pond Street. They ran together right round Hampstead Crescent into Rosslyn Hill and up to the police station and down Downshire Hill and round into East Heath Road and up by the rough wild national park of the heath across which over the centuries had blown so many other catalytic fevers.

"Can we—phew—slow down yet?" asked Caroline. Why was it always Alice on the bad days.

There was no sound of pursuit and they slowed to a kind of walk. The heath was lit by the fogged orange skyglow from

Highgate. She kept thinking of this seemingly normal man's waiting trainload of meat. Even now he still had his gun in his hand, waiting to kill.

She said: "This job's making you hard, Andy."

"That's what my wife says. You're both right, of course. When it's all over I shall go back to show jumping."

"Do you show jump? Daddy show jumped."

"My father was a famous show jumper in the thirties, Major Guy Fairfax?"

"Fairfax? Good lord! I didn't realise."

"He's got a duck farm now at Tonbridge Wells."

"Super."

"Not that way, miss." He was guiding her with the point of his gun. "They'll know your place. They've only got to pull out Elsie's finger nails. She treasures them. That's why she's no good at tossing off. Mind you, she'll never admit it."

Caroline looked at him in despair. The mind boggled. Captain Andy Turner was the absolute definitive man.

He said: "I know what. We'll go to Dobbin's. Dobbin's dead. They'll never think of that."

She said, probing into her worries: "And I can pick up his mother's address in Stevenage ..."

From Dobbin's room at the corner of Squire's Mount, half a person above the road level, they heard guitar and voice; the room was in darkness. The same song, the same young South African. They listened a moment, Andy holding her discreetly captive with one expert finger into her knicker top through the dress.

"Luras. Looma looma looma. In my hand,
I hold seed and plant and bloom. Ah,
In our love, we hold our future in the Rand ..."

"Raymond de Freitas," Caroline Latimer whispered.

"Hans knees and boomps a daisy. I don't trust him two yards." Captain Turner had checked his gun. Caroline grew depressed. "Try not to shoot anybody tonight."

The street lights suddenly came on, making them easy targets for hidden watchers at the window. Andy propelled Caroline up the steps of the house, pushed open the door into the dark hall. Now the music came, but fainter; they climbed five stairs and went in to Dobbin's shared flat, listening at his door. Guitar arpeggios through the tonic, the sub-dominant, the dominant seventh—tacit two beats and:

"Luras. Time to put your clothes on.
Your grandma, was raped by Paul Robeson ..."

Andy was about to open the door when Caroline said: "He's changed the words. Her grandma used to be raped by Baden Powell."

Andy said: "Are you sure, Caroline?"

She nodded.

He said: "Then he must have heard about the capitalist take-over. That means the Duke. That means a trap. Cover my back when I go in—now!"

Andy slowly turned the doorknob, then thrust the door wide open and sprang inside, his gun already firing. Caroline, close behind him, caught sight of Raymond sitting peacefully— luckily on the floor—by a lighted candle.

"Don't shoot him, Andy!"

The bearded, whimsical youth gave them his bright, Hans Andersen smile. "Hello, Ceptin Turner. Hello, Ceroline."

Another voice from the darkness behind the flung-back door, said: "Hello, Major Anthony Fairfax of the Durham Light Infantry."

Captain Andrew Turner, as he now called himself, remained stationary as if the name uttered meant nothing to him. This is a typically thick, army thing to do, Caroline Latimer had time to realise, for if the voice had said Rudyard Kipling under these particular circumstances it would have been more natural to turn and find out who had spoken. Caroline found out. There were two men, both with levelled revolvers. The one who had spoken and who had Andy covered she had not met before, yet he struck desperate chimes with terrorist newspaper and television pictures. The other was unmistakeably the canoist she had capsized by opening her legs at him while sunbathing on the boat. She blinked at him now and it unnerved him again. He took two strides like a bowler and punched her in the face, knocking her to the floor.

"Stay there, you cross-eyed piss-quick!"

This was an unwise move. Caroline Latimer had determined never to be hit again without killing. Lying on her back with blood coming from her nose, one contact lens lost forever, the bankruptcy examiner squinted her good eye and with two unbelievably fast shots hit both the assassins in the head, just behind the ear. As they fell, Andy sprang round, kicked their guns away, shot them both again.

"Good kid," he said to Caroline.

Captain Turner now turned his attention to the minstrel, raising his revolver again.

"Ceptin, no!" Raymond cried.

There was a banging on the ceiling and the bed-sitter boy lowered his voice: "No, Ceptin! Ceptin!"

Andy shot him instantly dead and put a second bullet through the guitar; an act which seemed quite elliptical to the graduate girl.

"For God's sake, Andy, that horrible canoeist was pointing a gun at him. He was forced to sing and play. You are a bloodthirsty bleeder, you really are."

Andy smiled and helped her to her feet, gave her a squeeze. "Oh, come on now. You're splitting hairs. Nobody could sing and enjoy it with a gun on him."

"Raymond could play through any—"

There came the thumping from above again and Andrew Turner put three fast shots where he judged it to be. It stopped.

"How many bullets does your gun hold?" she asked.

"This is another gun. I've four guns, three knives and some mini-grenades. Bit of cyanide." He yawned and scratched his chest under the leather jacket; the reason for his heavy clotes in such hot weather was apparent. He said: "How about turning in? You must be whacked."

"Do you mean—to sleep? With you? In Dobbin's bed? With all these corpses in the room?"

"You pull the bed together, Sergeant," he said. "I'll put 'em in the bath—" he detected her opposition by her solid unmoving stance. "Look, it won't be safe for either of us on the streets tonight." The accuracy of this had been already hinted at by the coming and going of police and ambulance thin siren screams in the summer night air. "Leave me a pillow and a blanket out. I'll take 'em in the kitchen—mind your feet, love."

She stood aside as Captain Turner dragged Raymond de Freitas away by his armpits. "I may want this blonde hair. It's the end of Captain Andrew Turner of Sycamore!"

Caroline Latimer sat on the edge of Dobbin's bed while her superior officer completed his tidying. As she was taking off a blanket and pillow for him she became aware of something dripping from the ceiling onto the sheets. The blood of some old lady upstairs, unable to sleep until now.

"Do you mind if I come in the kitchen with you?"

Andy turned at the door, his arms full of bedclothes. "Eh? Well, no skylarks now, Caroline. I'm a happily married man. That's what Elsie never understands. The importance of a Christian marriage, the family unit." They made up a bed together between the sink and the kitchen table and Caroline undressed, pulled the captain's boots off. "I slip her a length now and then of course, only fair. But only on that understanding. You girls are all the same. Independence, no demands on either side, but you all want the same thing in the end—security with a chap like me ..."

It was the last major dialogue of her screwrape experience and it bored Caroline to sleep. Sleep and dream. Security with a chap like Katy. Catherine Vesey while her Bonny was at sea, Norman when he wasn't, the baby all the time ...

God, or someone very much like him, threw a fistful of javelins in the following afternoon. The greatest electric storm of recorded weather struck the north London hills with water, ice and drums. Belsize turned into a sliding glacier, traffic lay marooned in Swiss Cottage, people drowned in their basement

flats, their hi-fi's swamped, lightning killed, housewives swam
into the Vale of Health, drains gushed their squalid secrets into
the air.

The early morning had held no promise that the heatwave
was sliding to its edge. When Caroline Latimer awoke and
came into Dobbin's living room, Andy, naked, great patches of
black hair amid livid scars of near misses, appeared to be doing
something painful to his red eye.

"Don't go," he said. "I may want you."

To take her eyes from his great balls and penis, at half-mast
even in repose, she rummaged in the sideboard drawer for
Dobbin's mother's address.

"Ouch!" said the Sycamore man. And "Oh, my God."

She was forced to look at him. To her horror the red
disfiguring birthmark came away in his hand. Next his ear
came off to reveal much smaller ones of different shape and
then the end of his nose, leaving a face—presumably the face of
Major Anthony Fairfax of the Durham Light Infantry—that
was quite unrecognisable. This stranger grinned at her.

"How do I look?"

"Awful. Ghastly. I'm sorry."

"That's all right. Soon think of something else. I've got this
friend in cosmetics. You're genuine, are you?"

She could only nod, apologetically.

He said: "We must team up again. You're a crack shot. I'll
see what I can do for you. You can always reach me through
Time Out. Small ad, sign it Caroline. Take your clothes off."

She said, "I've just dressed!" He needed them. "I'll wear
yours, you wear mine. No, that won't do. Still, you've got four
bodies to choose from—they're a bit smelly this morning." She
had noticed it; she had cleaned her teeth with a wet hanki
under the kitchen tap rather than brave the bathroom.

Caroline Latimer took off her knickers for the umpteenth
time and gave them to the officer. Andy put them on expertly,
holding his balls tight and wriggling his bottom until
comfortable. "What about a bosom?" she suggested.

He declined. "If you don't need one then I don't. Help me
with this skirt—you're not cold, are you? You're shivering.

She had just noticed Raymond de Freitas's scalp on the bed; or so it seemed. The long, blonde, wavy hair. "Lipstick and a bit of eyeblack, darling." Together they built him into a grotesque girl, the long hair stuck inside the canoeist's boating cap, the terrorist's sandals. She watched him practise his walk up and down the room. "There—how's that?"

"Fascinating." She noticed that he kept his legs shaved for moments like this.

"Well, good luck, kid. See you in the Ladies'!" He gave her a brief kiss and a friendly slap on her bare bottom, took a long, precautionary look out at the morning traffic, then left her.

She could not bring herself to call him Andy any more. Andy had already left her. She watched from between the white shutters until he appeared on the steps, saw him mince away, mingling with city workers, all hurrying away towards the tube. Soon she could not determine which of the women was Captain Turner of Sycamore. There was to be one picture postcard the following year postmarked Rhodesia.

Alone now, she grovelled on the carpet, searching in vain for her missing contact lens.

Later Caroline left the house and went across the heath, taking her direction from the green spires of Highgate. She wore the Hans Andersen denim shorts and shirt and not much else and carried her gun bag.

In a pretty sunlit glade by the path she sat on a log where many people have sat and from where it seemed you could see the whole of London, the high-rises shining like vertical mouth-organs, a ridge of Kent or Surrey woodland on the distant horizon. There were three distinct kind of grasses in diffferent colours and textures. Some was fine and pink and ripe with sprays of miniscule bell-like blossom, some parched and brown with the heat. And there was a patch chosen by rabbits who had left their little brown pills in clusters, where they had paused to crop the green and tender shoots into an undulating carpet pile. Wearing only one eye she found it hard to focus and as she sat there, squinting, her head to one side, she got the first inkling of an inkling for her book. A children's book, perhaps? *The Bunny Rabbit's Revenge*. Or, *Ben Bunny Gets His Own Back*. This is very often how social documentaries like *The Redundant Cock* are first conceived. She would have to put it to C.H.

"Good morning!"

Walking past her was a very pretty girl in a white summer dress, lots of dark hair hanging almost to her waist. It was Sweetie. Or Jennie. "Isn't it a nice day again?" she sang. Then, after a few paces, she looked back at Caroline, recognising her. "Oh! Did you find that chap?"

"Yes, thank you."

"And the other one who was chloroformed?"

"Yes, thank you."

"I am glad. I'll tell Petey. We couldn't sleep. Goodbye, Caroline."

"Goodbye," said Caroline Latimer.

She knew then that she would go on meeting the long weekend for the rest of her life. Saying hello and goodbye to its residents. A bee flew by on its perfectly steady journey and a nearby bird gave it a vulgar whistle. It was all going on. The mind positively boggled sometimes. What one must do was talk about it in some kind of official way and thus avoid getting certified. Perhaps one could make a living from it. Soon she walked on, full of fancies.